"I can't stand big, bossy men."

Dinah's admission to the big, bossy Marcus was a warning. Marcus responded with, "Is it being given orders that bothers you, or just big men?"

"The two together. Nobody likes being pushed around, but when big men start shoving I really dig my heels in." She looked into his tough, arrogant face, and was surprised to see him smile.

"Are you implying that I'm overweight?" he asked.

Perhaps, she thought, she was getting too personal. He looked hard-muscled, not overweight. She had been in his arms, and they had been anything but soft. "Well," she said, "the first time I saw you I thought you looked like a heavyweight boxer. But I'm a peaceful girl myself."

"Unless a big man orders you around," he confirmed with a laugh. "I'll remember that."

Jane Donnelly, a former journalist, lives in a picture-perfect cottage just outside of Stratford-upon-Avon with her daughter and their assortment of pets. She has written everything from short stories to movie scripts and has developed into a prolific author of warmhearted romance novels since she started to write for Harlequin in 1968. She finds her writer's life immensely satisfying, loves the excuse to travel and still has a reporter's instinct for gathering news and scribbling down notes, which she later uses in her books.

Books by Jane Donnelly

Don't miss any of our special offers. Write to us at the following address for information on our newest releases.

Harlequin Reader Service
901 Fuhrmann Blvd., P.O. Box 1397, Buffalo, NY 14240
Canadian address: P.O. Box 603,
Fort Erie, Ont. L2A 5X3

Fetters of Gold
Jane Donnelly

Harlequin Books

TORONTO • NEW YORK • LONDON
AMSTERDAM • PARIS • SYDNEY • HAMBURG
STOCKHOLM • ATHENS • TOKYO • MILAN

Original hardcover edition published in 1988
by Mills & Boon Limited

ISBN 0-373-02954-3

Harlequin Romance first edition January 1989

CHAPTER ONE

'I WANT to take you down to my home, where I can get you alone and unprotected,' Nicholas had said. 'And while you're there, you can meet my family.'

August had been a golden month. In every way, these last weeks had been some of the best that Dinah Marsden could remember, and she had no hesitation in saying, 'Yes, please, I'd like that.'

But when they arrived at the big white house, overlooking a cove on the Cornish coast, Dinah's bones were stiffening and her muscles were aching after ten hours on roads filled with cars and caravans, although the journey had had its compensations. She fancied Nicholas so much that being close to him was bliss, even on a hot day in a traffic jam.

When the car was at a standstill, he often put an arm around her. Sometimes they were delayed long enough to kiss and nibble ears, and that relieved the boredom— as well as getting wolf whistles from lorry drivers looking down on them through the open sunroof of their car!

But she was glad to hear, 'We're nearly there.' And the entrance drive, with tall gates and a small lodge, was imposing enough to make her gasp. So was the house. As she got out of the car, she looked up and around and whistled softly, 'Wow, how the other half lives!'

Nicholas laughed at their private joke and caught her hand, leading her between the white pillars into the entrance hall, with its wide, curving staircase and magnificent Persian carpets.

A man and a woman greeted them. Both middle-aged and obviously staff, Vera and Thomas seemed genuinely pleased to see Nicholas, and they both smiled politely at Dinah, eyeing her with frank curiosity. That was understandable, and she smiled back. 'Anyone else around?' Nicholas asked.

'Miss Thalia is sailing with the Tregarths,' said Vera, and in her mind's eye Dinah saw a magazine picture of beautiful people, cleaving through blue, foaming water on the deck of a gleaming white yacht. Miss Thalia would be as stunning as a model girl, with her hair streaming back in the wind. Vera added, 'The young lady's room is ready, if she'd like to come this way.'

Her thin little legs went like springs, giving her a bouncy walk as she tripped ahead of Dinah up the stairs. In a bedroom, she put down the case and asked if she should unpack, and Dinah said, 'Thank you, I'll do it.'

The contents of her case did not justify too much fuss. They were all right, but not, Dinah felt, up to the usual standard for guests in this house.

The bedroom was luxurious, with warm ivory walls and furniture, and it was a perfect summer's evening, but as she opened her case she gave an involuntary shiver, as if a dark shadow had fallen across her. Suddenly she was chilled to the bone, and she shook herself impatiently, because there was no reason for this.

She was here on a week's holiday, and if that was all it turned out to be she would be no worse off at the end of it. Her pride might be hurt, but she would hardly be destroyed, so that bleak foreboding made no sense. She got on with her unpacking, taking out her make-up case and putting it on the dressing-table next to the shoulder-bag she had carried herself.

That contained her precious Nikon camera that she rarely let out of her sight. At least she should get some good shots down here, so if her affair with Nicholas did peter out she would have the photographs to remember him by.

But that was pessimistic thinking, not her usual style at all, and now she washed in the little bathroom that led off her room, applying make-up with practised speed and changing into her most expensive dress. The turquoise blue silk had cost a crazy sum, but tonight she felt she owed it to her surroundings, which all around proclaimed a very high-class life-style.

Downstairs, Nicholas waited for her and they ate alone, served by Vera at a little table in a round window alcove overlooking the sea. Dinah had half expected Nicholas would want them to spend the night together, but as they got up after the meal he said, 'Get a good night's sleep, there's a lot I want to show you in the morning.'

He walked with her to the door of her bedroom, and in his arms she thought it was a pity to part. She looked up at him, eyes wide and lips curved. He kissed her then, stroking her cheek with his fingertips, and said, 'Goodnight, darling. You're here, and that's wonderful.' He added that it was late, and she was tired, and there was tomorrow and other days and nights.

So she said, 'Goodnight,' and hardly had time to stretch out between the cool sheets before she was in a dreamless slumber that lasted until Vera brought her morning tea. Dinah blinked in the sunshine that was filling the room.

She felt terrific, high with happiness, as she got into yellow flattie shoes and a shirt and skirt in brilliant yellows and greens and scarlets. She was a striking girl; her skin had the sheen of perfect health, and there was something vivid and zinging about her. This morning, with her hoop ear-rings, she thought she looked gypsyish, in spite of her swinging blonde hair, but her get-up matched her mood, which was at that moment all colour and gaiety.

Nicholas came up the stairs from the hall to meet her, telling her even before he reached her, 'You look fantastic.'

'So do you.' He looked boyish and happy, and she was completely rested and refreshed herself. 'I slept like the dead.'

'I know.' He slipped an arm around her waist and they walked down together. 'I came into your room and stood by your bed.'

'I wasn't lying with my mouth open, snoring, was I?'

'No, but you looked so comfortable I hadn't the heart to disturb you.'

She laughed. 'I wouldn't have minded.'

'I'll remember that.'

Looking at the furniture and the pictures this morning, she was certain that everything was genuine here. No copies, no fakes. No family, either. There were two places laid again at the little table by the window, and they had a magnificent view over the bay, with the sunlight glinting on the water and the cliffs rising sheer.

She sipped her coffee appreciatively. Good, strong coffee and a beautiful morning... Vera came in quietly, looking at Dinah with pursed lips. Maybe I'm too gaudy for her this morning, Dinah thought.

'You've got a lovely smile,' said Nicholas.

'Thank you. What happens today?'

'I thought we'd take it easy. Thalia should be back this evening, I want you to meet her. I don't know about Marc. He's in Amsterdam right now, so I'm not sure about him.' Marc and Thalia were brother and sister, Nicholas's cousins, and all the family he had.

'You're not sure if he'll be back, or if you want me to meet him?' she teased.

Nicholas said, 'Oh, you'll like him. But not too much!' And when her eyes widened, 'Remember I saw you first.'

'Am I likely to forget that?'

He smiled, turning it into a joke, getting up and fetching a silver-framed portrait from the top of a Regency writing-table. 'This is Thalia.'

'I'd have known her anywhere,' Dinah declared. She had the same chiselled features and full mouth as Nicholas, looking out from a cloud of red-gold hair. 'She's beautiful.'

'Yes, she is,' he agreed. 'I designed the jewellery for her twenty-first birthday. It's based on an old Cretan motif.' She was wearing ornate sapphire and gold earrings, and a low-cut dress that displayed a matching collar.

'That's beautiful, too.'

I doubt if we shall find much in common, Dinah thought, because Thalia had the expression of a sulky child, but she said, 'I shall look forward to meeting her.'

'I'll show you around,' said Nicholas enthusiastically.

Homes usually reveal the folk who live in them, and the tour of this house made Dinah feel that she knew Nicholas better. He had told her that his parents and his uncle had died in a plane crash fourteen years ago when he was twelve years old, and in the emptiness of this house, which had surely hardly changed, she could imagine the loss and the loneliness of the boy.

He took the luxury of the place for granted, leading her through the rooms that had her gasping, and it was only when they reached his studio that he smiled and said, 'Now, this is where I wanted to bring you. My workroom.'

It was a perfect room for an artist, overlooking the bay, light streaming in through the windows. On the white walls were two modern paintings, all swirling gemlike colours, and a reproduction of a fresco of Minoan dancing girls and flying birds.

There were photographs, too, a block of them making a display wall, and all featuring jewellery. Some were worn by models, some were pieces photographed alone, and Dinah asked, 'Yours?'

'Yes.'

There were other pieces in a glass-topped display case, and sketches on a drawing-board. 'It's gorgeous. All of it.'

Her interest was genuine, and not because she wanted to impress the man. She had an enquiring mind; 'born nosy', her father used to tease her. Most of the designs were inspired by the ancient glory of Greece, and Nicholas talked on, showing her the photographs and the display cabinet, telling her about the jewellery piece by piece.

'Let me get a picture,' she said. 'I want a shot of this room, and of you, of course.'

He smiled. 'You're an artist, too.'

But Dinah shook her head. She didn't create beauty; her photographs were more a search for truth. 'I'm not, but you most certainly are. You're lucky, having all this around you.'

She was referring to the studio, the house, the vista of sea and coastline through the wide windows.

'All this can have its drawbacks,' he said quietly, then he took a bracelet from the cabinet, a broad, heavy band of interlocking links. 'Do you like this one?'

'Incredible. Where's the fastener?'

It opened in his hands and he clasped it round her wrist, and again the join was invisible. She turned her arm around, peering closely. 'I give up. How do you get it off?'

'There's the trick.'

She held her wrist towards him. 'Well, show me. Or do it for me.'

'It's a present.'

'Is it gold?'

'Yes.'

'Then, thank you very much, but I can't possibly take it. It's much too valuable.'

Her refusal was firm, although she smiled, and he didn't argue. 'Well, you'll have to wear it today because I won't take it off, and by tonight you could have changed your mind.'

There was no reason not to humour him that far. 'I won't change my mind. But OK for today,' she said. 'I'll enjoy wearing it on loan, even if it does make my ear-rings look tatty.'

'We can find you ear-rings.'

'Please, no, this is quite enough responsibility!' She laughed. It was easy being with Nicholas, no effort at all. When they strolled out of the house, she could hear the laughter and voices of holidaymakers on the beach below. But he led her away from the gated steps which went down, and up a path to the clifftop, that was edged with brambles and cow parsley and wild roses.

This was private land although, as it was unfenced, trespassers must have popped up regularly. They passed a couple of teenagers who were doing no harm, ambling along in the sunshine, Walkmans clipped to waistbands and earphones over their heads. 'So long as they're not in the cockpit,' said Nicholas.

'Is that what it's called?'

There was a small, round building on an outcrop of clifftop. Inside, a stone seat ran round a wall, and open

windows overlooked the sea. 'There used to be glass in
the windows,' he said, 'but nowadays vandals smash it
so often, it isn't worth replacing. When there was glass
and there was a storm, it was like being in the cockpit
of a ship. I loved it as a kid, when the waves were crashing
up the cliff.'

'I can imagine.'

'I'm sure you can.' With his arm around her shoulders,
they both looked out. 'The last storm I saw from here,
Thalia and I crept out when we were supposed to be in
bed. I was thirteen, she's a year younger. It was just
starting up and I wasn't too keen, but Thalia was going
anyway.' That I can imagine, too, thought Dinah. She
looks like a girl who gets her own way.

Smiling at the memory he went on, 'When we got here,
it turned into one of the worst storms of the winter, and
we were both scared and trying to hide it.' He threw
back his head and laughed. 'Then Marc arrived and
frightened the pair of us out of our wits.'

She gave him a questioning glance, and he said, 'Of
course, you haven't met Marc yet. Well, to begin with
he's a big man, and he came roaring in out of the storm
and knocked our heads together.'

'Charming!'

'Then he frogmarched us back to the house.'

'Through the storm?'

'Right through it. There was a cliff fall that night—
it does happen—and it might not have been safe here.
We didn't come out in storms again. Marc laid down
the law about that, but the cockpit's always been one of
my favourite places. My father asked my mother to marry
him in here.'

'It's a romantic spot.' By moonlight, it would be even
more romantic. She would like to take pictures from the
cockpit by moonlight.

'It was a happy marriage. It lasted until they died. *My* marriage lasted two years.'

This was the first mention he had made of his marriage since that first afternoon and, before she could check herself, she was asking, 'What was she like?'

'Like Miss World, and not a bad actress.' His smile was twisted. He had been hurt, and reliving it wasn't helping.

Dinah resisted an impulse to put her arms around him and give him a big hug and tried to make him laugh instead. 'I once had a proposal up in the air. We were on one of those fairground rides and it broke down when we were right at the top, just him and me in a swinging chair, and he said, very seriously, "If we get down from here all right, will you marry me?" It was the "if" that put me off him. Not a man who looked on the bright side.'

Nicholas laughed. 'Have you had many proposals?'

'A few.'

'I'm sure you have.' He looked into her vivid face. 'Will you marry me?' and as her own laughter died away, 'I'm serious.'

'Ah!' she gasped. 'Well...' She was unprepared and stammering, and very glad to see the couple they had passed on the path loom up in the doorway.

They were still plugged into their music, both stick-insect thin, spiky-haired and wearing identical jeans and T-shirts. The girl was only slightly less flat-chested than her male companion, and they stared blankly at Dinah and Nicholas. Nicholas said coldly, 'This is private property.'

They lifted their earphones and the boy said, 'You what?'

'Be our guests,' said Nicholas.

'Yeah,' said the girl.

This was giving Dinah a few moments to get her mind together because, although it was much too soon to be talking about marriage, that *had* been a genuine proposal. On impulse, probably, but he meant it, and refusing the bracelet would be nothing to refusing the man. How she was going to do that without hurting him, she did not know, except by saying, 'Ask me again in about six months' time.'

'Bloody trespassers,' growled Nicholas, scuffing up the dust from the path as he strode off. The trespassers had watched them go, standing grinning in the doorway, and Dinah grinned back and waved. Nicholas said, 'For God's sake, don't encourage them.'

'Shall I take their pictures?' she teased, but he was not amused and he stopped suddenly in his tracks. 'They've no right to be here. Hey, you——'

'What's the blue flower?'

It grew in a clump near the cliff edge, and she didn't care what it was called, but she did not want the morning spoiled for anybody. There was space enough for four of them up here.

'I don't know,' replied Nicholas, then smiled at her because her ploy was obvious. 'We'll get it identified for you.'

He tugged a root loose, squatting down to get a grip, jerking it free as the ground gave way. Everything seemed to be in slow motion, so that even her scream was a drawn-out, mounting crescendo. She saw the earth move, a chunk of green-topped turf spreading out, cracking deep, and Nicholas thrown, arms wide, then slipping over. And she screamed and went on screaming, and the teenagers came running, and the girl was screaming, too.

'Keep back!' the young man was shouting, and Dinah took a couple of steps, then fell to her knees and crawled forwards. She heard the man yell 'Go to the house! Get somebody!' The girl ran, still screaming, and Dinah looked over the edge and saw Nicholas.

It had not been a sheer drop straight on to the rocks. He lay roughly half-way down on a ledge, and she called, 'I'm coming.'

'Stay here, you silly cow!' said the young man, who was already edging himself carefully down a little farther along. There were footholds, although it was risky going, and Dinah crawled along to follow him. 'Oh, God,' she prayed. 'Oh, God . . . no . . .'

'Don't *you* fall off the bloody cliff as well!' the young man screeched at her.

'I won't. Oh, God, let him be all right.'

She reached the ledge first, never looking down, going from foothold and handhold, and keeping her eyes on Nicholas, who never stirred. It could only have been a few minutes, but it seemed a lifetime, and she sobbed great, tearless sobs and heard nothing else.

When she touched him, the man behind her said, 'You'll roll him off, leave him alone.'

'I know.' She was crouched beside Nicholas now. She had his wrist and she could feel the threadlike pulsebeat. She looked across the crumpled body to the jean-clad teenager, and said, 'She has gone for help, hasn't she?'

'Sam? Course she has. You all right?'

'Yes.'

Sounds were reaching her now, shouts from below. Everyone on the beach was looking up, a mass of white, raised faces. Help would be coming, and she said, 'I'll stay here. Can you get back up and—organise things? You wouldn't be a doctor, would you?'

He gave her a fleeting grin. 'Garage mechanic.' He was white-lipped himself, 'But I know enough to know we shouldn't be moving him.'

Nicholas moaned, and she put gentle arms around
him, bending her face to his, whispering, 'Hush, my love,
it's all right. Just be still for a little while.'

The young man said 'I wouldn't have minded a nanny
like you!' 'Cheek!' said Dinah, then, 'Thanks.'

'That's all right. He'll be all right.'

Neither of them was sure of that, but she said, 'Thank
you,' again, and he got back to the top of the cliff, while
she stayed with Nicholas, who lay like a dead man. But
she talked to him until help came, and her role became
that of onlooker as coastguards and ambulancemen took
over.

Nicholas, strapped to a stretcher and still unconscious, was brought up the cliff and lifted into an ambulance. Her friends from the clifftop handed her her
camera, which they had picked up, and said goodbye
and good luck. The girl scribbled a phone number.
'You'll let us know how he gets on, then?' and Dinah
nodded mutely.

There were so many people around. She sat waiting
in the hospital with Vera and strangers. No one introduced themselves or asked who she was, and she sat
apart, not knowing who was here because of Nicholas
or for other reasons, other casualties.

The atmosphere was clinically brisk and chilling, and
it was a horrible day. One she would remember, shud-
dering, for the rest of her life. The interminable waiting
and then being told that she might as well leave because
she could do no good here.

She was getting nothing from the staff, it was all
coming to her through one of the others who had better
claims to be informed and consulted. Broken bones and
a head injury sounded so dreadful she dared not let
herself think about it. Then Vera, backed by a large lady
in a light tweed suit, came over to say they were leaving

and did Dinah want a lift? They would hear as soon as there was anything else to tell.

Nicholas was not going to die, that much she had learned, and she couldn't stay here indefinitely, so she said, 'Yes, please,' and sat in the back seat of the large lady's car until it drew up outside the white house on the cliffs.

The two women in the front did little talking. When they did, it was to each other, along the lines of what a terrible thing to happen, and how the dry summer was crumbling the coastline.

Dinah never found out who her travelling companion was, and when she got out of the car Vera stared for a moment, as if she had forgotten her. Then she gave a nervous twitch of a smile and walked off, leaving Dinah to follow.

Dinah was in shock. Deep enough to keep her quiet and still, and cold despite the warmth of the day. Thomas had come out of a side door to meet them and ask, 'How is he?' and Vera said, 'He's alive, when's the master coming?' And then they went into the kitchen, and Dinah walked on down the passage, reaching the big room where she had sat with Nicholas at the window overlooking the bay.

Nobody missed her, nobody looked for her. She felt numb and detached, as if all this was happening in a dream. She passed the portrait of Thalia and thought, you look a selfish little bitch; and she went to the table in the alcove and sat down, facing an empty chair.

It was her fault. She had sent him to the cliff's edge, picking that silly flower where the ground was crumbling. An accident that no one could foresee, but her fault. She slid a hand across the table, as if she could reach out and touch him.

She sat there a long time. Then went up to the room that was hers for now, and half packed her case, then left it because she didn't know if she would be going or staying. She found her way to the studio again and looked at all the jewellery, every separate piece, and at the bracelet on her arm.

If Nicholas was the only one who knew the trick of opening that, she might have to wear it until he could release her. And, if he wanted her to keep it, she would. If only he could be all right, she would do anything...

Several times she heard the phone ring, and each time she hurried to listen, standing in open doorways or on the gallery of the landing. Most of the callers had just heard about the accident and wanted to know how Nicholas was, and they were always told he was comfortable. Although how could a man who had fallen headfirst over a cliff be comfortable?

She stayed in the background, and nobody seemed to notice until Vera, answering the phone, looked up the stairs and said, 'Oh, there you are, miss. Can I get you something? You'll be wanting something to eat.'

'No, thank you,' said Dinah.

'I'll bring you something,' said Vera.

She vanished into the kitchen, emerging with a tray which she put on the little table by the window, darting off again while Dinah was still making vague gestures of protest.

She didn't seem able to get out the words, but no way could she eat. And her hands were sore. She had washed them at the hospital, but they were cut and grazed, although at the time she had hardly noticed that. Now she went to a bathroom and washed the cliff grime from her legs and feet, and swabbed knees and hands with a stinging disinfectant.

When she came downstairs again, there was a man at the window by the small, round table. The light was behind him and she remembered Nicholas saying, 'He's a big man.' So this had to be Marcus; standing there, he seemed to block out the sky.

She walked towards him as he stood waiting for her, and she gave her head a little shake to clear it. She had to pull herself together, but she walked slowly and he said, 'Miss——?'

He didn't seem to know her name, and she said, 'Dinah Marsden.'

'How do you do?' How did he expect her to be doing? 'I'm Marcus, Nic's cousin. Please sit down.'

He spoke courteously, but when she looked him in the face her breath caught. The family likeness to Nicholas was there, but older and much harsher. Lines ran across the brow and from nose to mouth. At some time the straight nose had been broken. That and the broad shoulders gave him the look of a heavyweight boxer. With the hooded eyes of a riverboat gambler, he was in every sense a formidable man.

'How is he?' she asked.

'Cracked ribs and slight concussion seem to be the limit of his injuries. It could have been worse.' His voice was deep and slow and controlled.

It could have been much worse, but she couldn't let go and whoop with relief, because there was a barrier of reserve in this man. He must have been concerned enough to get back from Amsterdam fast, but there was no offer here of a shoulder to cry on.

And she seemed to be emerging from her shocked state with a sharpened awareness. She did not like him. She would not have trusted him. She asked, 'When can I see him?'

'Not today.' Oh, he was the one who gave the orders...

'Marcus laid down the law...' Poor Nicholas, she thought. Between the pair of them, I wonder you can call your soul your own.

She kept her own voice as cool and controlled as his. '*You* will have seen him, of course?'

'Of course.'

He was still standing looking at her, and she knew he was not impressed. She said 'Then why can't I? You may be family, but I'm the girl he's asked to marry him.'

CHAPTER TWO

DINAH hadn't really meant to say that. But she very much wanted to get under his guard and, as the thick dark eyebrows rose, she thought—that shook you.

Then he was impassive again, drawling, 'This is rather sudden, isn't it? Dinah Marsden.' He seemed to be repeating the name, to see if it brought anything to mind. 'I can't recall Nic mentioning you. How long have you known each other?'

'A few weeks.'

It seemed longer, for they had slipped so easily into a close companionship. Dinah had been working, taking pictures at the opening of a country club. A fashion show was one of the highlights of the evening, and she was commissioned to photograph a couple of models who were wearing clothes from a local, upmarket boutique.

The buffet and the dancing and all the fun of a super party were perks of the job that night, but Dinah was a single-minded professional, and her attention was almost entirely on what she was seeing through the eye of her camera.

The models were all professionals too, incredibly beautiful and bony, wearing the *haute couture* clothes to the manner born, and photogenic from almost every angle. Dinah had stationed herself in a good spot, and every time Serena or Jix appeared she had clicked away. She was pretty sure she would have some good publicity shots, and she stood back to watch and enjoy the evening gowns that were rounding off the parade.

21

Neither of the girls she was here to photograph was in the final tableau. The dresses were beautifully cut but understated. It was the jewellery that had the audience goggling, and Dinah caught the eye of a young man who was leaning against the wall beside her. He smiled and she gasped, 'Are those rocks for real?'

'So they say,' he said, and she rolled her eyes.

'Wow! How the other half lives.'

The fashion show finished and the boutique owner who had commissioned her caught her and asked if she thought she had some good pictures, and when would they be ready? 'In the morning,' Dinah said. She took a few more for the fun of it, and left soon afterwards.

She had a busy day ahead tomorrow, and the sooner she could have tonight's photographs on Margot Manning's desk, the better. Her reputation as a free-lance rested on timing as well as talent.

She was not disappointed. The proofs had sparkle and style, and everyone was happy. By late afternoon, Dinah had dealt with her day's schedule and was finishing a cup of coffee, standing in the doorway between the studio and the reception area. Barbara, a plump, sweet-faced woman who had worked here for the last twenty years, was rearranging the photographs in the window, and when the door from the street opened it was Barbara who asked, 'Can I help you?'

'I want a photograph taken,' said the young man who had been watching the fashion show last night. He was so handsome that Barbara could not believe her luck. Customers like this were few and far between; he should photograph like a dream. She said 'Of course. Would you like to make an appointment? Or we could take your picture now. Mr——?'

She paused and he said, 'Christophi. Nicholas Christophi.'

He was looking at Dinah. Jewellery by Christophi, it had said on the bevel-edged invitations, and her lips curved while she pretended to be serious. 'I just thought they looked too good to be true.'

Barbara was puzzled, and Dinah explained, 'We met last night at Cheslyn Grange, and had a little chat about the jewellery in the fashion show. A family firm, is it?'

'That's right.'

'I didn't say it wasn't gorgeous.'

'The very word I've been looking for,' he said, staring her straight in the face.

The compliment was so direct that she laughed. She was not gorgeous, but she was fetching enough to turn heads, and she was flattered and delighted to meet Nicholas Christophi again.

'How did the pictures come out?' he asked. He had noticed her taking photographs and must have enquired who she was, because he surely hadn't strolled in here by chance.

'Not bad.' Sounding brisk and businesslike, her dark eyes dancing, she went on, 'Now, about this photograph you want. Mrs Coade does most of the studio work. She's *very* good.'

'Actually, I'm not wanting a studio photograph.' He had come in here to seek out Dinah, and all three of them knew it. 'Something out of doors, maybe?'

'What's it for?' Dinah went on with the pretence.

And Barbara chipped in archly, 'Or who's it for? Your wife?' She had seen the expensive car draw up outside and here was this fascinating young man, in pale blue silk shirt and trousers and cashmere sweater, looking as though he was born with a silver spoon in his mouth and had never been denied anything. He was after Dinah, and Barbara had misgivings.

'I'm not married.'

He looked at Dinah and she said, 'I'll get rid of this cup and get my camera.'

Barbara followed her into the studio, closing the door and declaring darkly, 'He wants no photograph taken. I know what he wants.'

'Do you, now?' Dinah teased. 'I think he's rather nice.'

'I didn't say he wasn't nice.' Barbara sighed and shrugged. 'Oh, well, you're old enough to look after yourself.'

'Yes, I am getting on.'

Dinah sounded exaggeratedly mournful, and Barbara had to smile.

'I only wish I was as young as you.'

Dinah was twenty-five. Sometimes she looked about sixteen, but when the going got grim she could look her age. Now she led the way out of the shop, and raised an eyebrow when he produced keys and unlocked the car. 'You don't see many of those parked in the high street,' she said, 'and you got a parking space just like that, right outside. Aren't you lucky? Where would you like this photograph taken?'

He opened the door for her, went round the car and joined her. 'The last thing I need is another photograph.'

She had guessed that. She said, 'You've never had one taken by me.' As it happens he had, but he didn't know that.

'Your photographs are special?'

She said gaily, 'But of course!' And they were. She put boundless energy and enthusiasm into her work, and she produced pictures that were always good and sometimes brilliant. 'So where do you suggest we go?'

He turned on the ignition and said, 'Away from here,' because a thoughtful-looking Barbara was standing in the doorway.

Dinah apologised. 'She doesn't usually enquire if our customers are married.'

'Well, I'm not. Not any more.'

She murmured automatically, 'I'm sorry,' although how could she be sorry?

'It was a mistake. Paid for and done with. Do you have any commitments?'

She played the field, happily and with good humour, breaking no hearts. Few men were prepared to take second place to a camera, and Dinah had to admit that she simply did not fall deeply in love. The heights of glory and the depths of despair had always eluded her, and she couldn't say she was missing them. She liked being in charge of her life and, although she could be impetuous, in the end her head always ruled her heart.

Nicholas Christophi was certainly one of the best-looking men she had dated, if this could be called a date, and when he smiled at her she felt a tingle that was a promising start. They were driving along the high street of the small Cotswold town, and she said, 'You don't live round here, do you?'

She had never heard of the Christophis, but that didn't mean they couldn't be comparatively local. There were lots of firms and families she didn't know.

'We've a home in Cornwall,' he told her, 'but we've just taken over an apartment at Cheslyn Grange. I'll be there for a while.'

That was good news, and she said, 'We?'

'There are three of us. Marcus, he's the head of the firm and the family. And Thalia.' He said that name with a smile. She didn't know how he felt about Marcus, but there was no doubt that he was fond of Thalia. 'She's a character.'

'Your sister?'

'They're my cousins, but we grew up together. And what about you? Are there any more at home?'

'No,' she said. 'My mother died a long time ago, my father last year.'

The name over the shop still read 'Anthony Marsden', and it was still hard to believe that he was not somewhere around, in the house or the studio or the darkroom, the quiet, gentle man who had loved her.

Nicholas drove with no particular aim, taking country lanes through picture-postcard villages of black and white thatched cottages as they talked, getting to know each other; and all the time her liking for him grew. When they stopped for a meal, in a small hotel called the Old Mill, with the millstream foaming beneath its windows, she was already feeling that she had found a friend, maybe a lover. She disliked macho males who swaggered around giving orders. Nicholas was amusing, he made her laugh, but he seemed sensitive and understanding, and she was not surprised to learn that he was an artist. Some of the pieces worn last night had been his creations.

When they parted, quite late, he kissed her and arranged to see her next day. Alone in the ground-floor bedsitter that was now her home, she took out the photograph she had taken of him last night.

She had always found she could learn more from photographs than from flesh and blood faces. Her photographs, even shots like this, where the victims had no idea they were the subject, often seemed to capture the essence of the personality. Reach the soul, as it were. That could be why her love affairs petered out. Because she took pictures of the men in her life that revealed too much.

This study of Nicholas showed him listening to a fat man who had obviously downed more than his share of free champagne. Nicholas was bored but hiding it, yet his mouth had a weary line. Fair hair, almost silvery under the bright lights, flopped over his forehead.

He looked vulnerable and her heart went out to him. From the outward signs, he was a man who had everything, but the impression stayed with her that Nicholas Christophi needed friends.

Every time they met she liked him more, and that month they often met, eating out, seeing shows, taking trips here and there. But there were usually others around, and sitting in a crowded restaurant Nicholas had said, 'I want to take you down to my home, where I can get you alone and unprotected.' He'd squeezed her hand and leered so that she got the giggles. Then he added. 'And while you're there, you can meet the family.'

Now she was facing head-of-the-family Marcus, who was demanding, 'And when did he ask you to marry him?' It might have been a professional interview, he could have been checking her out for a job in the firm.

Irritated, she snapped, 'Why don't you ask him that?' But, when he waited, she said, 'This morning.'

He indicated the empty chair at the table.

'May I join you?'

The last thing she wanted was to sit down with him, especially if he was proposing they should eat together. But he didn't need her permission to sit at his own table, and she murmured, 'Why not?'

There was a salad bowl on the tray, fruit, cheese, a slice of pie and an opened bottle of wine. Now that she knew it was not too bad with Nicholas she *should* eat, even if she had no appetite, and she would not for the world let this man overawe her.

She helped herself to salad while he poured wine into the glass for her, going to a cupboard for another glass, telling her, 'He's coming home tomorrow, and there'll be a nurse for a few days. From tomorrow, of course, you can see each other as often as you wish, but he's under sedation now, resting.' He took bread and cheese and said drily, 'One way and another, I feel he's had enough excitement for today.'

So had Dinah. Her nervous system had been shocked rigid. Everything had been marvellous and then, in seconds, so awful, and there had been nobody to turn to who cared how she was feeling. Even now, she was straining to keep her voice and her hands steady.

She had no transport. Getting a taxi and demanding to see Nicholas would be more stress, and she wasn't sure she was up to it yet. And he would be out of hospital tomorrow.

She said, 'Yes, all right, I'll wait.'

'So, where did you meet?' Questions again, in that deep, implacable voice.

'At the opening of a country club. Cheslyn Grange. I was taking photographs. I'm a free-lance photographer. Do you want your photograph taken?'

She had no idea why she said that and he said, of course, 'No, thank you.'

Now she saw what they meant by a smile that didn't reach the eyes, and she thought, you could beat me, I could take a photograph of you that would tell me nothing. 'What did happen this morning?' he asked.

That was something she did not wish to think about, and she said quietly, 'The cliff crumbled at the edge. He was—picking a flower for me.'

'A charming gesture. He's always had a romantic streak.'

It was obvious what he thought about that, and she wished she could think of something clever to say.

She was managing to eat a little, leaving her wine almost untouched. It was as though she owed it to Nic to stay on her guard here. He had asked her to be his wife and it was possible that some day they might marry. Right now, she felt that he needed her just to stand by him and stand up for him, and she said 'He's a brilliant designer. The jewellery's exquisite.'

'I see you appreciate it.'

The bracelet was conspicuous on her slim, lightly tanned wrist, and she wasn't trying to hide it. Why should she? However, she knew Marcus knew its value and thought she had accepted the gift. 'I can't get it off,' she said.

'Shall I?'

She looked at his hands. They looked strong and well shaped, the skin tanned dark against the narrow, white strip of shirt beneath the slate-grey jacket, and she did not want them touching her. Her arm had been resting on the table and she drew it away, slipping both hands into her lap and folding them together.

'Don't bother,' she said. 'Nic will tell me the combination.' They were so different, these cousins, and she heard herself say, 'You're older than he is?'

'Much older.' And not just in years. Nic was an artist, a dreamer, but this was a man of action who looked as if he had packed in every experience you could name.

It made her dizzy just thinking of the kind of life he must lead, and she said the first thing that came into her head. 'Thalia's very beautiful.'

That seemed to surprise him. 'You've met her?'

'I saw the photograph. Nic thought she would be back today. You were in Amsterdam?'

'I was in London.'

'Then he was mistaken.'

'He can be.'

He clearly thought that wanting to marry her was a mistake, and she said crisply, 'Can't we all?'

'Yes, indeed. You live near Chesford?'

'Yes.'

'You have a family there?'

'No.' She sat back and looked challengingly at him. 'Look, Nic knows all about me and he can ask any questions he likes, but I'd rather not be interrogated by you. You wouldn't be his guardian, would you? And even if you are, he's a big boy now.'

'Is that how I'm sounding?' The first real smile she had seen softened the hard face, so that it was not so difficult to understand why Nic had said, 'You'll like him.' She could imagine him being a charmer when it suited him, but he was not charming her.

'That's how it sounds,' she said.

'I apologize. I'm not Nic's guardian—I'm not quite that old—but I am interested in the girl he's going to marry.'

He was taking it for granted she had accepted, and there was no other way she would get any status in this house. She couldn't leave here until she knew for sure that Nic was all right. Nearly losing him had brought out a fierce protectiveness in her.

She said, 'You're not married?' Although Nic would surely have mentioned that.

'No.'

'Then why don't you concentrate on your own love-life?'

'I do. I give it a great deal of attention.' And her lips twitched in an unwilling smile. She bet he stopped well short of commitment, but some women would find him very attractive. Power was supposed to be a big aphrodisiac, and he was a powerful man. But for Dinah it was a turn-off. Men of power were usually bullies, and more than one promising relationship had ended when a man started ordering her around.

But he had charisma. As they carried on with their meal, she became less tense. They talked about Nic; he had always been an artist, Marc told her. Christophi jewellery had been a family business for generations. The family originally lived on one of the Greek islands, but forty years ago two brothers who were educated in England had settled here, married, bought this house. And died together in the plane crash.

She told him then that she had lost her parents, about her work, and how Nic had come round to the studio the day after the opening of the country club. After a while, she was doing most of the talking, but she had nothing to hide and perhaps she had over-reacted, resenting him in the first place.

She had no reason for believing he was not unbiased and caring in his dealings with Nic. Any more than she knew that Thalia was spoiled and selfish. Maybe the last thing that Nic needed was protecting from his family, and when she met Thalia she would find she was a very nice girl.

But when Thalia Christophi *did* arrive, it was obvious that 'nice' was not the word for her.

Dinah and Marc were still sitting at the little table as Thalia came into the room. Night was falling by now, the big room was in shadow. Marc got up, turning on a light in the alcove, telling his sister, 'We've got a visitor. A friend of Nic's.'

'Of course,' said Thalia.

Dinah felt like someone spotlit on a stage, although when Thalia came closer she thought that, if a spotlight was on anybody here, it would be on Thalia. She would have been the star. She looked like one of those pre-Raphaelite paintings, with her rippling mass of red hair and her sullen beauty.

She sat down, facing Dinah in the seat Marc had just vacated, and asked, 'Were you with him when he fell?'

The questioning again, without any pretence at friendliness. 'Yes,' said Dinah.

'What was he *doing* on the cliff edge?'

'Picking a flower,' said Dinah.

Marcus said, 'He didn't tell you that?'

So Thalia had been with Nicholas all this time, although he was resting and sedated and Dinah was expected to wait till morning.

'He didn't tell me anything,' Thalia said. 'He still can't remember anything, but he's going to be all right and he's coming out tomorrow.'

'What can't he remember?' Dinah leaned forward as she asked Thalia, but it was Marcus who answered.

'The fall and before it. But you knew that.'

'No, I didn't. What does it mean?' The words jerked out. 'It doesn't mean he's got brain damage?'

'No.' He sounded confident, reassuring, and she breathed again as he went on, 'Blocking out what led up to an accident is a common type of memory loss. It's usually temporary.' But he watched her as if he meant to catch any change of expression, even the slightest muscle twitch.

Thalia's laugh was harsh. 'You wouldn't have pushed him off the cliff, would you?'

I don't like you either, Dinah thought, and she said what she felt would wipe the smirk off Thalia's face. 'He asked me to marry him this morning. I wonder if he remembers that.'

Thalia did stop smiling. Her eyes seemed to darken, and Dinah almost flinched from the naked hatred in them. 'I shouldn't think so,' said Thalia.

'Do you think I invented it?' Thalia shrugged and Dinah turned towards Marc.

He thought she'd known that Nicholas had amnesia, but who would take such a gamble? Where would be the sense in it? And he said, 'Why should you? It would be a ridiculous thing to do.'

'Wouldn't it?' said Thalia. 'But then, Nic usually picks the ones who don't miss a trick.'

So Nic had a losing streak in relationships; probably he was taken advantage of because he was easy-going. He would not be the first man like that in Dinah's life. Her father had been too trusting for his own good. She had looked after his interests for years.

Now she said, 'Then we'll have to wait till tomorrow, won't we? I'm sure he'll remember if he wants me to go or stay.'

Thalia had seen the bracelet. She stared at it, arching perfect brows, then she drawled, 'Or we could just say now—how much?'

Marcus said sharply, 'That's enough,' and to Dinah, 'I apologise again. This has been a trying time for everybody.'

He had shut Thalia up as if she was being tiresome rather than unforgivably offensive, and Dinah said, 'I'll take myself off.' She went out of the room quickly, to stop herself demanding, who the hell do you two think you are?

It would be ironic if Nic never did remember proposing to her. That would surely rate as her oddest proposal, crazier than the one at the top of the fairground wheel. 'Will you marry me?' he said, and fell off the cliff. Not that it would matter if he couldn't remember, because she hadn't accepted. But Thalia wanted to believe that Dinah was trying to trap him and could be bought off.

And, in spite of what he'd said, it would not greatly surprise Marcus. He was watching her very closely to see if she was acting, pretending that she hadn't known about the amnesia, and he had been encouraging her to talk during the last hour or so. She had told him a lot about herself, much much more than he had told her. He had managed the cross-questioning so skilfully that she had hardly noticed it. Talk about the smile on the face of the tiger!

At least Thalia was open about what she was—spoiled rotten—but charm and courtesy could almost hide the fact that Marcus Christophi was a ruthless man.

She stayed in her room after that. Although lights were on all over the house now, she only opened her bedroom door once and looked out, then changed her mind about going downstairs. Nobody down there wanted her company, and she was too exhausted to take them on again.

Her hands and knees were smarting again, and a hot bath might have been painful, or might have relaxed her. She unpacked her half-packed case, and replaced her clothes in drawers and cupboards, because she would be staying on for the rest of the week. Then she took her time washing and getting ready for bed.

Today had shattered her, leaving her reeling. She sat up with the pillows piled behind her, turning the bracelet round on her wrist, trying to figure how to get it off, because it seemed to be growing heavier by the minute.

But her eyes were closing and she felt too stupid to solve anything, a puzzle for a six-year-old would have fazed her. She let her arm drop down beside her and let the bedside light burn on. It was twenty years since she had slept with a nightlight, but she did not want to be alone and in darkness in this house.

For what seemed hours, she tossed restlessly before she fell into a troubled sleep, and even then she must have been aware of the unfamiliar weight of the bracelet.

She dreamed she struck it loose, banging it against a rock as high as a mountain, and was immediately caught again and held. But this time it was not a golden fetter, but a man's hand encircling her wrist. Marcus Christophi gripped her, and she thrashed around in such panic that she nearly threw herself out of bed.

She woke on the edge of the large bed. She could understand her subconscious wanting to get rid of the bracelet, but what did the rest mean?

She tried to lie quietly, playing the game of interpreting a dream to get the nightmare into perspective. A little mental exercise to calm her mind.

It probably meant that she thought he would try to stop her doing something she wanted to do. Like looking after Nic right now, keeping him safe and happy. She thought he would try to stop that. Her instincts told her that Marcus might put obstacles in her way.

The dream could be explained, but it had produced a rather disturbing fact: sleeping or waking, she couldn't keep Marcus Christophi out of her mind.

CHAPTER THREE

THE knocking on the door woke Dinah next morning, and then the rattling of the doorknob, and Vera calling 'Miss? Are you awake, miss?' as if this was not the first time of asking. Dinah surfaced from a deep sleep. The last thing she remembered was switching off the bedside lamp because dawn was streaking the skies, and then she must have slipped into her first sound slumber.

Bleary-eyed, she opened the door on Vera and a tea tray. 'Glad you had a good night,' said Vera, faintly reproachful. She obviously thought that Dinah had slept without a care from the moment her head had touched the pillow. Dinah took the tray and asked, 'Is there any more news?'

'He'll be back this morning.'

Vera was not hanging about gossiping, but she did look round as she moved away to say, 'Oh, congratulations, miss.'

'Thank you.'

'Funny, him not remembering, isn't it?' said Vera, and she was off down the corridor, although she need not have rushed because Dinah had no reply to that. It was fairly hilarious if anybody thought she was dumb enough to invent a marriage proposal. 'Nic usually picks the ones who don't miss a trick,' Thalia had said and Dinah wondered, like what? Some time, she might ask him to tell her about these 'tricky' ladies!

This morning she was herself again. She gulped a little of the hot tea, brushed her hair and made up her face, then slipped into a white linen dress, knotting a black

36

and white spotted silk scarf around her throat. Her natural resilience had asserted itself, and no one in this house was putting her down today. If Thalia made any more cracks about paying her off, that young lady would hear some home truths.

Marcus was crossing the hall when she came downstairs. 'Good morning,' he said. 'Did you sleep well?'

She could hardly say no, when it was after ten o'clock, so she said, 'Yes, thank you. When will Nic be home?'

'Around midday.'

'How is he this morning?'

'No complications.' He added laconically, 'Medically speaking.'

She took that up. 'Would I be a complication?'

'I hope not.' Which meant he thought she was going to be a nuisance. Well, that was just too bad. She was Nic's friend. She would keep out of the way of the rest as much as possible, but she meant to be around when Nic came home.

She walked out of the house into the sunshine and down the gated track to the beach. Down there, the bay was filling with holidaymakers, and she wandered barefoot along the water's edge, turning away from the house and the evidence of the earth fall. Looking up at the jagged cliff edge against the skyline, and down at the fallen turf among the rocks, made her feel sick, but when she turned her back on it it was easier to stop brooding on what might have happened.

Nic had escaped with minor injuries and she was thankful for that. And it was pleasant down here, with everyone enjoying themselves, splashing in the sea, sprawled out on the sand, children running and playing.

She called at a seafront café for coffee and a round of toast and honey. If she had asked for breakfast back at the house she would probably have been told by Vera,

'You're too late, breakfast's finished.' Here, she sat at the little table, drinking her coffee, almost feeling part of the holiday crowds.

She could still see the white house; it overlooked the whole bay, but there was a small hotel down here and a few guest houses, and she longed to walk into one of them and ask for a room. She did not want to go back. She wanted to see Nic, of course, but Thalia would probably be just as spiteful this morning, and the autocratic presence of Marcus Christophi loomed ominously.

But she was convinced that Nic needed her. And, besides, she had left her camera behind, so she couldn't run away. She grinned wryly at her own joke, and a young man who had been trying to catch her eye for the last five minutes thought he had cracked it, and beamed back, and was left goggling when she got up and strode past him.

She hadn't even noticed him, but she had decided she had no excuse for lingering longer. Nic would be arriving home soon, and she made her way along the beach to the gated path, then slipped on her shoes and trudged up to the house again. All the doors seemed to be open, and she walked between the white pillars through the main door into the hall.

Thalia came out of a room, asking abruptly, 'Where have you been?'

So abruptly, in fact, that Dinah snapped, 'To the beach. Should I have asked permission?'

'This is Gordon.' There was a young man with Thalia, bespectacled, and studious-looking. She threw him a slanting smile. 'See what I mean?' she said. He tried to cover his embarrassment by babbling, 'Gordon Fowler, how do you do? Another beautiful day, isn't it?'

Yesterday hadn't been so beautiful, in spite of the sunshine, but what Thalia had been telling him about Dinah had obviously disconcerted him.

'Nic's back,' said Thalia, and Dinah couldn't conceal her disappointment, because she had wanted to be here when he arrived.

'You shouldn't have swanned off,' said Thalia smugly.

'How is he?'

'Shaky.'

'Can I see him?'

'Can we stop you?'

'No.'

'So come on, then,' said Thalia and led the way upstairs.

Nic was in a big room, a bedroom, although he was sitting with his feet up on a long settee by the window. He was fully dressed, wearing an open-necked shirt, an arm in plaster and still with a yellowish tinge under the tan of his skin. He looked, as Thalia had said, shaky.

'Carolyn's here,' said Thalia, standing back to let Dinah walk in. 'Whoops, sorry, this one's Dinah, isn't it?'

'Don't be childish,' said Nicholas, and he held out a hand for Dinah. 'Hello, darling. It's good to see you.'

She went quickly across to him and he gripped her fingers, lifting them to his lips. 'It's good to see you,' she said.

Thalia had flounced away, and there was no one else in the room, so she stooped to kiss him. The last time she had done this had been on the cliff face, when she had not known if he would ever open his eyes again. Now he was warm and alive, and she was filled with joy and tenderness. 'Poor love,' she said. 'You gave us such a fright.'

'I gave myself a fright, too.' She sat on her heels beside the settee, holding one of his hands in both hers. 'I came round in the ambulance,' he said. 'Then I blacked out again. They tell me I slipped over the cliff.' She nodded and he asked, 'What happened?'

'You were pulling up the root of a flower, and the turf gave way.' His mouth fell open as if that was news to him. 'What do you remember?'

Concentration creased his forehead. He said softly, with pauses, 'Breakfast. Then bits and pieces. Being in my studio. It's all very hazy and mixed up.'

'Do you remember taking me up to the cockpit?'

The frown deepened with the extra effort, but he said at last, 'No.'

'Telling me your father asked your mother to marry him in there?'

'No. But he did.'

'So you won't remember asking me to marry you?'

The blankest look yet followed that; this had to be the first he had heard of it since the accident. Then he grinned ruefully, 'What a husband you'd be getting, a man who forgets he proposed!'

'True,' she said, 'so let's go back a bit. You remember I'm supposed to be on a week's holiday here? Do you want me to stay on?'

There was no hesitation there. His *'Yes,'* was prompt and emphatic. 'It's only yesterday I'm confused about. I remember very well why I wanted you to come down here.'

'To get me alone and unprotected, and so that I could meet your family,' she said gaily.

'Right.'

'Well, I've met them.' She found herself loosing his hand and turning the bracelet on her wrist. 'They weren't expecting me, and they didn't like me.'

He'd have gathered that from Thalia, just now if not sooner, and he sighed, 'It wasn't how I planned it. I thought you could meet and get to know each other gradually. What happened?'

'Who will you have first?' She sat back on her heels. 'I think Thalia's the best. Thalia thinks I made up the bit about you proposing, but she did offer to buy me off.'

She was smiling, although she had not found it amusing and she still didn't. But Nic grinned, as if it was a joke, advising her, 'Ah, take no notice. She'd say that to shock you, and if she managed to see you off that would suit her. She always has some bloke in tow, but she likes to keep me as her bachelor brother. We're good mates, almost like twins. Marc's ten years older than me, very much our big brother.'

He saw no wrong in either of them, and she said crisply, 'Big brother wasn't impressed with me, either.'

'I'm sorry.' He looked at her fondly. 'But you'll win him round.'

'I wouldn't bank on that.' She couldn't see a girl twisting Marcus Christophi round her little finger, and she couldn't see herself trying, asking to be humiliated. But Nic wanted Marc to like her, and he wanted her to make allowances for Thalia's appalling behaviour. Family affection gave them a strong hold on him. She asked, 'Do you need his approval?'

'For what?'

'The way you live.' She shrugged. 'Your love-life. Anything. I mean, if he's the head of the firm, could he cut you off without a penny?'

She grimaced at the melodramatic turn of phrase and Nic said, 'Of course not.'

'Well, I'll try not to cause any trouble. More than that, I can't promise.' She was glad that Nic was not de-

pendent on Marc's good will and, because he did look
fragile she asked gently, 'Does your head hurt?'

'Only when I shake it.' His grin was wan. 'Or think
too hard.'

'Don't think, then. Just try to rest.'

In the silence she heard voices, a woman's and the
unmistakable, deep, slow tones of Marcus. Still sitting
on her heels, she turned so that she was facing the open
door when they reached it.

The nurse came in first, wearing a blue uniform dress
instead of the jacket and skirt she had worn yesterday
at the hospital. She was the large lady who had given
Dinah a lift back, and now she was smiling and friendlier,
greeting Dinah. 'Good morning, our patient doesn't look
too bad, does he?'

Our patient could have looked a whole lot better, although Dinah said, 'He looks fine,' and Marcus raised
a quizzical eyebrow. She would have liked to add that
he was bound to look better compared to how he looked
when she was half-way down that cliff, and she'd thought
he was dead—just for Marcus's benefit. But that would
have been morbid talk, and done the patient no good at
all.

She got off her knees, drew herself to her full height
and looked away from Marcus, giving her attention to
Nic and the nurse. It was medicine time. The nurse was
handing him little white pills and a glass of water to help
them down. He swallowed and then she took his pulse.

He said, 'I'll go downstairs. I can manage that.'

'I'm sure you could,' said the nurse, releasing his wrist.
'But for today I'd rather have you in here. That was a
very nasty knock you took.'

Nic's beautiful mouth set stubbornly, 'No, I shall go
down. I can take things just as easily downstairs.'

The nurse began to protest, 'Well, if you want to know my opinion...'

Clearly, he did not, until Marcus said, 'Stay where you are. There's no point in taking unnecessary risks.'

Then he muttered, 'Oh, all right,' without any further argument, although his expression was as sulky as Thalia's.

The nurse looked relieved, and Dinah asked sweetly, 'May I stay?'

She addressed herself to Marcus, who seemed to be making the decisions in here, but he looked at the nurse, who said, 'Well, yes, as long as you don't overtire him.'

Dinah opened her eyes wide. 'What do you think we might get up to?'

The nurse chuckled. 'Not much, with him with two cracked ribs.' She was in a cheery mood now her authority had been upheld. She went over to a desk at the far end of the room, and made a note in a notebook there. Marcus was standing near, and she continued a conversation she had been having with him as they walked along the corridor together, about getting somebody a job. 'As I was saying, my sister's boy is a good lad, and if you could see your way to giving him a chance...'

He asked a few questions, concerning age, qualifications, and so on, reminding Dinah of last night when he'd been questioning her. She smiled at Nicholas, who whispered, 'I should have woken you on Saturday morning.'

'You missed your chance there,' she breathed in his ear. Both Marcus and the nurse were speaking quietly, and it was a big room, so they should have been out of earshot of whispers. But Dinah suddenly felt that Marcus could hear her. And that he knew what she had said before he came into this room. She felt he had extra keenness of hearing and sight, almost ESP, something that made the small hairs stand up on the back of her neck and jerked her head round.

He was looking at her. He was listening to the nurse, taking in what she was saying, but his eyes were on Dinah, who felt her throat go dry.

'I love you,' Nic murmured, and she turned back.

'Tell him you asked me to marry you.'

'Now?'

'Please.'

He took her hand, kept his eyes on her face, cleared his throat and blurted, 'I've asked Dinah to marry me.'

The nurse gave a little trill of surprise, and Marc said, 'So she tells us.' Nicholas gulped again, his Adam's apple bobbing in his throat. 'Memory coming back?' Marc enquired pleasantly.

'Oh, I remember that,' said Nicholas, and Dinah heard the quickness and the defensiveness that made even the nurse look thoughtful. Marc, she was sure, knew it for a lie.

She held out the wrist with the bracelet, asking, 'Do you remember how to get this off? Do you remember putting it on?'

'Not too clearly.' Nic sounded tired, and he closed his eyes, but behind the lids he was trying to reconstruct the scene. 'I remember being in my studio, and you saying something about the bracelet making your ear-rings look tatty.'

She was still wearing the cheap gilt hoops. They swung against her cheeks as Marcus drawled, 'Couldn't you have found some matching ear-rings?'

She wanted to shake her head and say, 'It wasn't like that.'

'I can't remember,' said Nic, and it was no good prompting him or protesting that she'd said she didn't want any ear-rings and she'd only wear this on loan.

'Would you get it off, please?' she asked. One hand was in plaster. 'Or tell me how.'

Marc came and took her hand, and she wished she had said nothing until he was out of this room. She should have known this would happen, and it was the hardest thing to stand still and not pull away, because she felt every light touch and pressure of his fingers deep inside her. When the heavy gold links fell apart, she realised that she had been holding her breath, and let it out in a long sigh.

Marcus slipped the bracelet into his pocket, and as he believed it had been a gift he had no right to do that. Her lips parted to say, 'That is mine.' But she didn't want it, Nic couldn't remember, and she was not looking for a confrontation with Marcus.

'Take care not to lose it,' she said sweetly. 'I'm sure it's very valuable. These are more my kind of thing.'

She flipped an ear-ring and Nicholas winced. 'Those are *tat* and you are a classy lady, you underestimate yourself. Doesn't she?' he asked Marcus.

'I doubt it,' he replied, so affably that both Nic and the nurse imagined he was somehow paying her a compliment, and smiled, too.

Dinah's expression showed what she thought. She glared briefly at him, managing to convey that she did not give a damn for his opinion, on her or on anything else. But she had not meant to let him get under her skin, and she turned away at once, as he said to the nurse, 'Tell David that if he rings here, I'll see him tomorrow.'

'I'll phone and tell my sister, and thank you,' said the nurse.

They both went out, and Nic said, 'Of course he likes you.' Dinah couldn't believe her ears! But it was what Nic wanted to believe, and she went along with it.

'Maybe. So long as you do, that's the main thing. Should you be resting? Do those pills make you drowsy?'

'I feel shattered.' There were a couple of newspapers on the desk and he said, 'You know what I'd like? I'd like you to read to me. You've got a very sexy voice.'

'I have?' That made her laugh, she hadn't been told that before. She went over and collected the papers, scanning the headlines. 'I can't promise to make this lot sound sexy.'

Nicholas grinned and leaned back and closed his eyes again. 'Cut out the heavy stuff,' he said, 'and find me something soothing.'

She took the brighter, lighter paper, and sat down by the window, turning the pages, looking at pictures first. She always did that, for some of her own photographs had appeared in the nationals. When she came to the gossip columns, she gasped, 'It's you! This is about you.'

Nicholas's face looked up at her from the page, with the caption, 'Over the Top.' She read, 'Jewellery designer Nicholas Christophi, twenty-six, fell from the clifftop in the grounds of his Cornish home on Sunday, and is now nursing broken bones. More bad luck for Nic, who was briefly wed to starlet Carolyn Hayes.'

She paused, and Nicholas said, 'Find something else.' A cliff fall was news, and so were the Christophis. Dinah had not realised just what that family firm entailed until her eyes skimmed on. ' . . . Cousin, entrepreneur Marcus Christophi, whose interests range from Christophi jewellery to a two-million holiday village in a tropical pearling port.'

'Do you want to see it?' she asked.

'I never bother with the scandal page.' She had never met anyone before who would not have snatched a paper the moment they heard they were in it and devoured every word. But the Christophis obviously got enough personal publicity to be blasé about it.

She asked, 'Where's the holiday village?'

'Which one?' He sounded bored.

'It doesn't matter,' she murmured, and turned back to page one and started to read out the headlines. She kept her voice low and soothing, then found a feature on wildlife conservation, and when the nurse came back Nic was asleep, with Dinah providing the lullaby.

'Do him good,' said the nurse. 'Better to leave him now.' There was no reason for Dinah to go on reading, but she wondered if Marcus might have said, once outside this room, that he would prefer her visits to be kept short.

She would look in again in an hour or two, but for now she went meekly enough. Anyhow, she wanted to phone Barbara. Someone was bound to see that photograph and wonder what was going on, and she picked up a phone in an alcove off the hall.

There was no dialling tone. Instead, she heard a man give a phone number, and then Marcus said, 'Jack? Marc here.' This was certainly none of her business, but she stood with the phone pressed to her ear, because there was something almost hypnotic about his voice.

He was giving somebody instructions about a property development that he had probably been handling in London when Nic thought he was in Amsterdam, and she would have put the phone down, except that a click could have betrayed a listener. This could have been commercial espionage, if she had had a clue what it was all about.

The other man said, 'Right, I've got that.' And then he asked, 'How's Nic?'

'He's home now,' said Marcus, 'and we have a problem that will need careful handling if it isn't going to develop into another Carolyn situation.'

The other man's exclamation drowned Dinah's gasp, and now she really listened, but she learned nothing because the man said, 'God forbid! I'll get on to this right away.'

'Do that,' said Marcus. 'I'll be seeing you.' And the phone went dead. But she still replaced hers gingerly, and when a door opened along the hall and Marcus came out of the room she shrank back in the alcove.

Luckily, he didn't come her way. She might have found it hard to act as if she had just reached the phone, pick it up and start dialling. Another Carolyn situation, was she? A problem that needed careful handling?

Right, she thought, watching his broad departing back, let's see how you propose handling me, boyo! Let's find out how you handled Carolyn.

She rang the shop and got Barbara, who knew nothing about Nic's accident and was horrified. 'Where were you when this happened? You're all right, aren't you?'

'I was way back. He went to the edge of the cliff.'

'If the place is slipping into the sea,' said Barbara, 'I think you should be coming home!' And Dinah had her first real laugh for ages.

'Oh, course it isn't! Only little bits are falling off round the edges. No, I'm fine, and he's going to be, but it is in the papers and I thought I'd better warn you.'

'Hmm,' said Barbara. 'Some holiday.'

'Well, the sun's still shining,' said Dinah, 'and it *is* beautiful down here. I'll be back at the weekend.'

She didn't think anyone was listening, but one never knew. She had done a lot of eavesdropping on phone calls herself since she had come into this house.

'That's nice, I suppose,' said Barbara. 'You take care of yourself.'

'I will,' Dinah promised, and wondered how Barbara would react if she had added that she'd better, because one spoiled brat of a girl and one very powerful man were out to get her.

The house was not buzzing, but it no longer felt empty, the way it had before the accident. There was music. She could hear a Barbra Streisand song and voices when she stood listening in the hall. Marcus had gone towards the back of the house and the kitchens, the music and voices came from the big drawing-room and were probably Thalia and friends.

Thalia and friends Dinah could do without, and she went back upstairs to her bedroom and fetched her camera. It was one of her friends, a familiar companion. She never felt alone with a camera, and she took a long-shot photograph of the coastline through a window. It was a lovely house. Whatever the future held, she would like a record of it, and she wandered around, snapping whatever took her fancy.

Like Vera. Mischief seized her when she saw Vera tripping towards her, and she said 'Smile, please.' Vera jerked back in surprise, as if Dinah was levelling a gun at her head.

'I want to take your photograph,' said Dinah.

Vera didn't find that very reassuring. She didn't smile, but she stood still and stared while Dinah pressed the shutter and said, 'Thank you.' Then Vera scuttled off, obviously intent on telling them that Nicholas's latest girlfriend was running amok with a camera, because a few minutes later Thalia came looking for her.

Dinah was almost enjoying herself. Working was one thing that could blot out her worries, and for a moment her mind was occupied with the pictures she was taking. She was in a booklined room, concentrating on one corner and a leather armchair, when Thalia walked in.

She saw Thalia. When she breathed deeply, she caught a whiff of Thalia's perfume, but she took her picture before she turned towards her and Thalia asked, 'What *are* you doing? Preparing a guide-book?'

In a way, Dinah was, although it was unlikely that anyone else would see these pictures; they were just for her own eyes.

She said, 'I'm a photographer, that's my job. I guess it's my hobby, too. I do it all the time.' But this was an invasion of privacy, and she was sure that Thalia was going to say, 'Not here, you don't.' When she asked, 'Does Marc know?' that amounted to the same thing.

'No,' Dinah admitted.

'Then, if I were you, I'd get his permission,' said Thalia, 'and no, Nic won't do. It wouldn't occur to Nic that a record of this place could fall into the wrong hands.'

It should have occurred to Dinah. She was taking pictures showing fabulous items and a layout of the house. She said, 'Sorry, I didn't think of that.'

'No,' Thalia drawled, 'you wouldn't.' And she didn't mean because Dinah was obviously honest, but because she was too thick to consider the implications. She looked at her now with open contempt. 'Why don't you go down to the beach again and take some holiday snaps? You should keep in your hand, because you're still going to need your job. And if you've been taking pictures in here and thinking all this will be yours, forget it.'

Thalia hated her. She thought that Dinah was greedy for what she deemed her own property, her bachelor brother, the magnificent contents of her home. Thalia was the greedy one and Dinah would have liked to say, I bet you were a grabber in your cradle. But she had just made a fool of herself, and she was in no position to start trading insults. So she said, 'Yes, I will go down to the beach again. I could do with some fresh air.'

The house was air-conditioned, but Thalia's malice was oppressive, and for the second time that day Dinah walked away from a Christophi and couldn't get outside fast enough.

This time she took the clifftop path past the cockpit, walking her frustrations away, reaching the next cove and using up energy by keeping moving. Thalia made her angry, which was, of course, what she'd meant to do. But Marcus was the one to be reckoned with. She had never met anyone before who gave her the impression of holding so much in reserve. A tip-of-the-iceberg character, capable of lord knew what.

He would have made a good Roman emperor—Tiberius, maybe. Sitting high above the arena in his purple-edged toga, giving the thumbs-down signal to the gladiators, so that some poor so-and-so got the chop. And that was what he planned for her. The chop. Not literally, of course. Just a quiet, quick exit from Nic's life.

But it wasn't that funny. She didn't think Nic would appreciate the joke, and there wasn't anyone else she could tell it to.

On her way, she finished the film with a couple of photographs from the cockpit. A man had asked her to marry him here and, although she had not given her answer, it had already changed her life. Yesterday's horror was fresh in her mind, and she remembered the girl putting a phone number into her hand and saying, 'You'll let us know, won't you?'

She had no idea what she had done with that scrap of paper, and when she came out of the little summer-house she looked around as if it might still be lying on the turf on the clifftop. There was litter, crisp and cigarette packets, empty drink cans, but if she had dropped the note it had fluttered away. She could have slipped it into the pocket of her skirt. She'd check, and if she could find it she would ring and tell them that Nic was home now, and say thank you again.

When she got back to the house, she went up to Nic's room. He had visitors, only four of them including Thalia, but there was so much laughing going on that the room seemed crowded.

Nic was still on the sofa by the window, and a short, skinny young man with dark, bushy hair was tapping a front tooth and saying, 'And then this cap dropped into the curry.'

His account of dental disaster, which seemed to have been going on for some time, had them howling. He was obviously a favourite comic, and above the laughter Dinah heard Thalia say, 'Nic, you're starting to look tired. We'd better get out.'

She had seen Dinah in the doorway. Nic had not and he said, 'It was good to see you.' The nurse bustled up, agreeing that it was time they went. She was smiling, but visiting hours were over and her smile faltered as Dinah said, 'Hello, darling,' to Nic.

'Where have you been?' Nic's tone was plaintive.

'I told you,' said Thalia. 'Down to the beach.'

Dinah felt guilty. She supposed she should have stayed near. As soon as she was clear of the house, Thalia had probably dashed straight up here to tell him, 'She's swanned off again.'

Now, Dinah could only say, 'Sorry, I'll stay put now,' but the nurse insisted that Nic should be resting, and Dinah was ushered out of the room with the others.

In the corridor, Thalia said in an offhand fashion, 'This is Dinah. Gordon you know, Jake and Filly,' and they all said hello very casually, and went on talking among themselves, moving off in a group.

Dinah wondered what Thalia had told them about her. That she was a nobody whom Nic had brought down for the weekend? But not, Dinah thought, that he had asked her to marry him. Thalia did not believe that, and could well be hoping that soon Dinah would go away and the whole unpleasant affair would be forgotten.

Dinah was almost wishing that herself. Thoughts of her friends and her work, and even her little bedsitter, made her homesick. Here, she was being harassed and humiliated, but Nic was here and he needed her, so running away was impossible.

She searched for the scrap of paper with the phone number without success, and was annoyed with herself for losing it, although yesterday she had been in such a state she could have mislaid anything.

Downstairs, Vera told her that a place was laid for her tea, and she found herself sitting alone at an oval, rosewood table in a small room, being served with sandwiches, cakes and tea.

Thalia seemed to have left the house with her friends, and there was no further sign of Marcus. During the rest of the afternoon, Dinah took a book from the shelves in the booklined room. It was a thriller by a writer who was a household name, and inscribed, 'To Marc, with thanks for your help.'

What help, she wondered? And as she read on into the plot of sex and skulduggery, she thought, with research, no doubt. I bet he could have written this book himself!

She was almost sure he was not here, although she did not ask about him. She read her book and looked in on Nic, who was sleeping still. She spent time in the bedroom allotted to her, but wherever she was in that house she could sense the presence of Marcus. Other folk appeared, but Dinah was apart from their comings and goings, sitting quietly in the background, especially during the evening meal.

Thalia was at the table, and Gordon, along with another couple—a Dr Marsh and his wife Ellen, who seemed at home. And Marcus. Most of the conversation went over Dinah's head. She knew neither the people nor the places they talked about, and when she was drawn in—never by Thalia—it broke the easy flow of dinner-table chat.

She kept her remarks brief, and then they could all ignore her again for the next twenty minutes. She could have put on a better show, for she was bright enough to sparkle round any table, but with Marcus sitting there she was saying as little as possible, and after the meal, when they went into the drawing-room, she excused herself.

Nobody asked why she wasn't joining them. She murmured, 'Would you excuse me?' and got smiles from the visitors and dismissive nods from the family. She left them in the hall and went upstairs.

There was another man in with Nic when Dinah tapped on his door. 'Come in, darling,' Nic called. 'Come and meet Jack.' The man got up out of his chair and she went through the motions of yet another introduction. This had to be the man Marcus was talking to on the phone, she recognised his voice, and she was not hanging around to be inspected by him. So she smiled and said,

'I just looked in to say goodnight, and I'll see you tomorrow.'

'I'll be up and about tomorrow,' Nic declared, but the nurse was discouraging.

'We'll see about that,' she remarked.

Dinah went on her way alone, and sat at her bedroom window, watching night fall until the moon, a great silver globe, hung over a magical land. She longed for Nicholas, so that they could walk together down there, arms around each other, through the shadowed, scented night.

The little summer-house, high above the sea, would be like an enchanted tower. It was a time for lovers, and she felt utterly alone. When her father had died she had experienced a terrible loneliness, but that was bereavement. This was a yearning for a lover, regret for a wasted and a beautiful night. But at least she could capture some of the romance, and she put a film in her camera with a colour-correction filter over the lens and, using a tripod, she took another photograph from the window.

Although it was quite late, she was not tired, and, when she was in the cockpit yesterday, she had promised herself some shots of that scene by moonlight. There was no danger. It was nearly as light as day. She would take a torch, and she was not going near the cliff edge.

Sneaking out of the house gave her a childish thrill of triumph. If she wanted to walk by moonlight, that was her choice, but she could imagine Thalia shrilling, 'Taking photographs on the cliffs, at this time of night? You're mad!' She might even be forbidden to go, held back, but she dodged them and she drew great gulps of the cool night air deep into her lungs before climbing up the track, taking no risks, but still hurrying.

Almost as if—and this made her smile when the idea came into her head—she was meeting her lover up there. Well, make-believe was fun. She could see the pale stone of the cockpit, and she went eagerly and sure-footed over the outcrop of rock, playing her game of pretence, by imagining that he would be waiting.

The little room was empty. Just as well, because there was no chance of Nic being here, and trespassers might have turned ugly. But tomorrow she would tell him that she had been back and that she had pretended he was with her. She would have the photographs to prove it, and if he scolded she would say, 'The moon was so bright, it was like an evening stroll.'

She set up her tripod and took her pictures over the sea, and then sat down on the stone seat that ran round the walls, looking out through the glassless windows. She could happily sit here dreaming, but if she did there was a good chance she would be locked out of the house. If that happened, she thought she would prefer to doss down outside rather than get anyone up to let her in.

It would be nice if Nic was downstairs tomorrow. It would be nice if Marcus went away. If she knew for sure that he had gone back to London, or Amsterdam, or wherever, she might rid herself of the feeling that any time she turned her head he could be right behind her.

She turned then, looking inland across the little outcrop and shut her eyes tight, but when she opened them he was still there. Or maybe it was some other man, as tall and broad-shouldered; whoever it was, he was walking towards the cockpit.

Idiotically, she looked around for somewhere to hide, and then she had to suppress an equally insane urge to rush out and run. Of course, there was nothing she could do but sit and wait. He could see her. Moonlight streamed through all the windows and the gaping doorway, and either an almighty coincidence had brought him here, or he knew where she was.

As he reached the doorway, she said, 'Am I bugged with a tracker device?'

'Nothing so dramatic. I saw you leaving the house.'

There were a lot of windows and, with the moonlight and torchlight, her light clothing must have been easy to spot. She had her camera case slung over her shoulder, so it wasn't necessary to say, 'I've been taking photographs,' but she did, and asked, 'It's all right photographing out here, isn't it?' Thalia would have reported that she had been photographing in the house.

'Of course.' He practically filled the doorway. When he came in and sat opposite her, he seemed to fill the little room. 'I hear you're good,' he said.

'Who told you that? Nic?'

'He'd be prejudiced.'

For an unbiased opinion, he would have to ask someone else, and she snapped, 'You've been vetting me.'

'It wasn't hard. Your life seems to be a fairly open book.'

He was making her sound as dull as ditchwater. 'But I still don't fit the bill?' she said coldly, and he answered her question with another.

'You know about Nic's marriage?'

'Just that it didn't last. And that her name was Carolyn.'

She felt disloyal, discussing Nic like this with anyone, but Marcus had to know much more than she did, so she wasn't betraying any confidences.

'That's about it,' he said. 'She was an actress of sorts. She married Nic for his money.'

The lack of any sort of emotion in his voice shocked her, and she demanded, 'How would *you* know?'

'Because she told him, and in economics she was no child. She took him for enough money to set up a string of beauty shops.'

Now he sounded almost amused and she said fervently, 'Oh, poor Nic!'

'Hardly,' he said. 'But he couldn't afford to make the same mistake again.'

Before she could stop herself, she muttered, 'Another Carolyn situation?'

'God forbid!' he snapped, repeating the words Jack had used on the phone. Now he certainly suspected she had been eavesdropping, and the dark was not enough to shield her from those piercing eyes.

But she managed to keep her voice steady. 'For your files, if you've opened one on me, I'm not after Nic's money. That is, if he's got any left after Carolyn.'

For some reason, that made him smile. He said, 'He has a great deal left, which is common knowledge. And for a woman whose man could have been seriously injured, you seemed remarkably casual yesterday.'

'What?'

'You didn't insist on seeing him. You were quite prepared to wait until he came home. You lost no sleep, and today you've been out of the house most of the time.'

She couldn't explain. He would not understand how shock and everybody disapproving of you could make you quiet and wary. He looked used to riding roughshod and making his own rules. She said doggedly, 'I think he needs me.'

'There we differ.' Of course they did. They probably differed on anything one could name. 'But being apart for a while should prove something.'

At the end of the week they would part, but she could get back down here. And the Christophis had an apartment in Cheslyn Grange, and there were always hotels, places to meet. She said, 'We need not be so far apart. I'm fairly mobile in my job.'

'Where he goes, you go?' He was mocking her, she knew.

'More or less.'

'He'll be leaving for Styros in the next few days.'

'Where's that?'

'An island off Crete.'

She said incredulously, 'Are you shipping him out, to keep him away from me?'

'You mean, kidnapping him? Hardly. This time of year, we often go there. There's an old villa up in the mountains where we used to spend holidays when we were children. It's a good place to convalesce.'

She challenged him. 'Suppose Nic asked me to go with him, would you stop that?'

'Nic can invite anyone, of course, but I would prefer it if you left him alone for a few weeks.'

'Or even months?' Was he going to make her an offer now? 'Did you follow me out here to have this little talk?'

'And to make sure you didn't take the wrong path. Another accident so soon could give the place a bad name.'

'Very considerate,' she said tartly. 'You do make a smashing host.' The darkness was all around them, and the memory of her dream came back. She thought, if he touches me I could start screaming. She scrambled to her feet. 'I'm going back. I've taken my pictures.'

She darted through the door and set off, walking too fast. Striding out as though she was on a broad highway was asking for trouble, especially with camera, tripod and torch. Inevitably, she lurched on the uneven ground and Marcus grabbed her. His hands clamped down on her shoulders, whirling her round towards him, so that her face was crushed against his chest. She was being enveloped, smothered. She threw back her head; his face was a fraction above hers and she met his eyes, panting like a cornered animal. But in seconds he wasn't holding her any more. 'If you slowed down, you'd reduce the risk of falling flat on your face,' he drawled.

That made her sound an idiot, but her heart was still thumping and she said, 'It's turned chilly,' and she was off again.

This time, she kept her eyes on the track, but she still made the distance back to the house in record time. It was only when she reached the door that she stopped and fumbled with the latch, which seemed to be sticking.

'Allow me.' He reached across, and she jerked back as though the latch had turned red-hot. He opened the door and light flooded out of the house.

She said, with a gaiety that sounded hysterical, 'There must be a knack to it.'

He thought she was a fool—he didn't need to say so. But she went right on, 'I'm not usually clumsy. Nor stupid. I don't think you're only sending Nic to Styros for his health's sake.'

His voice was quiet and deep, and he could have been laughing at her. 'Far from underestimating yourself, you imagine you're more important than you are.'

'Who doesn't?' she said. 'Goodnight.' And she hurried off towards the stairs and her bedroom.

She must stop rushing and talking rubbish, but Marcus Christophi made her jittery. He did not want her to marry Nic, but he did not consider she was that much of a problem. Nothing he couldn't handle. Starting by parting them. Sending Nic off to this island in the sun, while Dinah went back to her little town in the Cotswolds. It was maddening to know it was all so easy for him.

She might try to persuade Nic not to go, but why shouldn't he? She couldn't say that it was better here or

that she couldn't bear to let him out of her sight. That
was ridiculous. This was the thin end of the wedge that
Marcus hoped would lead to a permanent parting. But
it was intensely frustrating to have to stand by meekly
and let it happen.

Unless she went, too. With a little planning, she might.
This week had been the first holiday she had taken this
year, and if she went home and began organising she
might get away again.

She wanted to be near Nic while he was convalescing,
and help look after him. Marcus had said that of course
Nic could invite anyone, although he had added, 'I would
prefer it if you left him alone for a few weeks.'

That had been nearly an order, and a miscalculation
on his part, because she did not take orders. She would
love to tell him in the morning that she was sorry, but
she'd be there.

In the morning, Nic looked brighter. When Dinah
tapped on his door and the nurse opened it, he was
dressed, shaved, sitting at the window drinking coffee.
He got up and came to meet her, moving carefully, but
walking well enough, and she said, 'You look better.'

The nurse said, 'I think we'll cure him,' and tactfully
left the room as he put his good arm around Dinah.
With cracked ribs, there was no question of hugging,
and she reached out and cupped his face in her hands
and gently kissed his mouth.

Looking up at him, she remembered Marcus's dark
face and the weight of his hands on her shoulders, and
she said, 'Marcus says you're going away to one of the
Greek islands.'

'Styros. I'm thinking about it, yes.'

'When?'

'Any time.'

'Is it beautiful?'

'Very. Any chance of you coming?'

She said, 'I've been thinking about that too.' He started to smile, the smile widening as she went on, 'I'd have to go back home first, of course, but I might be able to arrange things so that I could fly out and join you for a week or two.'

'But that would be marvellous!' And this time he managed to kiss her quite satisfactorily, and they began to plan.

Ten minutes later, they went downstairs. They would have breakfast together, and then the sooner Dinah left for home the sooner she would be free to fly out to the island. It would take her a little while, for there were commissions she had to fulfil, so Nic would be waiting for her. He took her arm going down the stairs, but he didn't really need supporting. When they walked into the little room off the hall, where Marcus and Thalia were sitting at the table, eating breakfast, Thalia said, 'And what's put the smile on your face?'

'Dinah,' said Nic, taking a seat.

'Silly question,' said Thalia. She had a couple of opened letters on the table beside her. Marcus was reading a newspaper.

'Dinah's coming to Styros,' Nic announced. 'I've been telling her about it.' And his smile was for Dinah as she sat down beside him.

'Fabulous,' said Thalia, with a cynical twist to her mouth.

Marcus said nothing. If his expression showed anything, it was faint boredom, and yet, this should have been a little triumph for Dinah. She had been convinced he would be annoyed that she was following Nic. So, surely she was mistaken to start wondering now if she had played right into his hands and done exactly what he wanted her to do?

CHAPTER FOUR

DINAH came to the villa when night was falling. Her journey from home had not been trouble-free and, although this helicopter flight over a dark blue sea, dotted with boats and islands, should have been exhilarating, she was too tried to enjoy it.

It would have been different if Nic had met her at Heraklion. She had expected to see him when she came through customs in a flood of chattering, excited tourists, clutching her camera case and her battered suitcase. She had wandered around for some time and then thought, that's it, he hasn't had my message, this is definitely not my day.

So, what should she do? Take a taxi and find somewhere to stay for the night? Tomorrow, she could try to make contact and finish her journey, but she was not risking any more bad luck today.

Then a man said, 'Miss Marsden?' He was a stranger, thick-set and middle-aged, clearly sent to meet her.

She asked, 'Is Nicholas all right?'

White teeth flashed beneath a heavy black moustache. 'He is making excellent progress.'

Then why wasn't he here? She had come a long way, but she was glad to see the stranger who picked up her case, which was swaddled with webbing straps, so that it looked like a badly packed parcel. 'My car had a bump on the way to the airport,' she explained, and he gestured shock and sympathy, and loaded both her and her case into a car parked alongside the tour buses and taxis.

Later, another man was beside her, at the controls of the helicopter. He was pointing downwards, nodding and smiling and saying, 'Styros.' She could see boats in the harbour, and the houses looking like little boxes, then the dark green of the groves and, among the hills, clusters of villages. Flying lower, they passed between mountain gorges and, as they dropped from the sky and the ground came rushing up to meet them, she closed her eyes. She was feeling queasy. She loved flying, her first helicopter trip had been smooth, and she would be in Nic's arms in a few minutes, but the strains of the day were telling.

The helicopter settled like some unwieldy bird, and the pilot came round to help her down. She stood, swaying a little. A wide terrace ran from the helicopter pad, and the man coming down the steps was Marcus. The air seemed to be full of a sickly perfume, and she went towards the house, asking as she reached him, 'Where's Nic?'

'Excuse me a moment,' he said, then spoke to the pilot. She didn't recognise the language, so it was probably Greek. She went up the marble steps, through an archway, into a courtyard open to the sky where a fountain played, statues stood in alcoves and a great purple wistaria rose high as an oak tree.

The perfume in here was softer, not so overpowering, but then the other odour came at her again; Marcus had followed her, carrying her suitcase. She asked once more, 'Where's Nic?'

However, he looked at her battered case and asked, 'What happened here?'

'It was on my way to the airport. A car ran into the back of me.' Coming off a roundabout at Milton Keynes, a car in front of her had braked suddenly. She had managed to stop in time, but the car following had gone smack into her boot, leaving her dear little Mini a write-off, concertinaing her suitcase.

It had looked at first as if she would never catch her flight, but she had had a smattering of belated good luck. A nearby garage towed her car away, jacked open the boot and lifted out her luggage, then hired her a taxi for the next twenty miles. Nobody was hurt. She exchanged insurance details with the other driver, and reached Luton as her plane was announced for boarding. There followed a dash to the airport shop to buy an armful of luggage straps, securing the case as best she could and running with it to get her boarding-card and hand the case over.

She was the last passenger up the steps, and when she had time to think she needed a double brandy, because she had filled up with petrol before she set off, and if the impact had struck a spark the smashed tank would have gone up like a bomb. When she got back, the hassle would be waiting for her, but it was remembering her narrow escape that was giving her the shakes.

'You weren't hurt?' Marcus sounded concerned, but anybody would, told of an accident.

Dinah said quite heartily, 'Not at all. Nor was the other fellow, and his car only had a little dent in the front. He actually drove it away, which seemed a bit unfair, as it was his fault. Where's Nic? We aren't alone here, are we?'

She was giving that just the right light note, but she was a little apprehensive, and when he said, 'If you don't count the staff, yes,' she jerked around. 'Nic and Thalia left before your call got through,' he went on. 'Nic's having a medical check-up in Rhodes. It's all right, they'll be back tomorrow.'

That meant she would be alone tonight, in this house in the mountains with a man with whom she could never relax. What she would do was plead exhaustion and ask to be shown her room, then stay there till morning. Tonight, she was risking nothing. Tonight, like today, could be a bad scene. She asked, 'Could I see my room?'

That was no trouble. He opened a door off the courtyard, and there was a bedroom with cool, black marble floors, and windows latticed in scrolled iron. Nobody could get in through those windows, she thought, and knew she was insane to imagine for one moment that Marcus Christophi would consider climbing through her windows or breaking down her door! 'I think you'd better open this,' he said.

This was her case, lying on the floor, with a pungent, sickly smell rising from it like a cloud. She put her purse and camera down, and knelt and started unclipping the safety-straps one after the other, until they lay in heaps around the case. The locks were jammed, but that didn't matter because the lid had burst open, sides and back, and she lifted it gingerly and groaned, 'Oh, God!'

If she had been able to empty and repack right away, there would not have been this spoilage, but there had been no cases of any kind for sale in the airport shop, and she had not had a minute to spare. Everything smashable seemed to have smashed: suntan oil, dark and viscous, skin creams, shampoo, baby oil, perfume. During the journey, they had soaked slowly through layers of clothing, finally leaking their way out when the case was unloaded just now.

Everything could be ruined. She should have known it might be, but she had hardly thought about the case again. Once sealed, she had just hoped for the best, although now she said, 'Pity the Customs didn't decide to inspect it,' and took out a shoe that did not seem to be stained.

Nor was it, but the heel was snapped and, as she knelt there holding it, she could feel the tears trickling down her cheeks. She couldn't stop them and she was bitterly ashamed, because this was the last man in the world in front of whom she wanted to break down. She ducked her head and began to delve, and a sliver of glass pierced a finger. With a cry, she held her fingers in the other hand, watching the welling of blood.

'Sorry,' she said. 'Only I've had a ghastly time, trying to fix things to get here. I've been rushing around ever since I left Cornwall, working all hours.'

She pulled out the sliver of glass and was sucking her finger but she couldn't check the flow of words. 'I'm just tired, I guess. I only heard about the flight yesterday. I was on stand-by, and when I got into my car this morning I thought, now it's all going to be marvellous, just wonderful. And then I write my car off, and here I am with a case full of stuff that looks as if it's been dredged up from an oil well. What's going to be next, do you think? Do you believe in things going in threes? What unbelievable thing is going to happen to me next?'

'You could lose your voice.' He said it gently, smiling, and she rubbed her cheeks with the back of her hand and got to her feet.

She needed the support of a hand beneath her elbow, and then, when he gathered her close, she knew that she needed comforting too. For a few blessed moments more she went on crying, and it did her the world of good. She could never remember crying like this in front of somebody else, with strong arms around her. She had only ever cried alone since her parents died.

She didn't look up at him. She simply rested against him and let his strength flow into her until the tears stopped and what had seemed like the final straw became

no more than a hell of a nuisance. Later, in the telling,
it would be good for a laugh, and she began to smile
wryly now. 'Thank goodness I didn't put my camera and
gadget bag in the boot of the car!'

'Looking at that,' he said, 'you've plenty to be
thankful for. You say the car's a write-off?'

'If ever I saw one. A garage towed it away for me.
They got me a taxi, and I was being paged at Luton. I
was the last passenger, and this,' she indicated the heap
on the floor, 'was the last piece of luggage in the hold.'
She moved away from him almost reluctantly, going
closer and peering down. 'What *do* I do now?' she asked.
'Shall I leave it to settle till morning?'

He went to the door and called, 'Ireni!' Almost immediately a young woman appeared. She was wearing a
plain dark dress, and her glossy hair fell in a thick plait
to her waist. When she smiled, she was pretty, and
Marcus said, 'Deal with it, would you? Miss Marsden
was in a car accident.'

The smile went, replaced with horror. 'Oh, madam!
You were hurt?'

'I'm fine,' said Dinah, although after her flood of tears
she had to be looking ragged.

'She will be fine,' said Marcus, 'when she has eaten
and rested.' And tomorrow she would be her usual, in-
dependent self, but right now she was glad to let
somebody else take over.

She said, 'Be careful, there's broken glass,' and held
out her nicked finger.

Ireni said, 'I will take care.'

Marcus said, 'Come on,' and his arm around her
seemed natural as she went with him out of this room,
across the courtyard, into another.

On a white and gold dressing-table were bottles and
jars, perfumes, cosmetics, and he slid aside doors, re-

vealing rows of clothes. 'You should find what you need in here,' he said. The largest bottle was the perfume Thalia used, and Dinah said, 'Thalia's?'

'Yes.'

Her sense of humour was returning. 'No, thank you. Thalia thinks I've got my claws into too much of her property already. If she came back and found me decked out in her clothes, she would be less than delighted.'

He smiled. 'Chance it,' he said. 'I'll take the responsibility.'

'Well, I suppose it couldn't hurt to use her bathroom.' Through an open door, she glimpsed azure marble that looked cool and inviting, when she was hot and sticky and grubby.

Marcus said, 'I'll see you in—half an hour?'

'By then I'll be a different woman,' she said gaily, and she thought he might even have said, 'Not too different.' But it was hardly a murmur above the sound of footsteps—another woman had appeared in the doorway to the courtyard.

She was about three times the age and girth of Ireni, but enough like her to be her mother or grandmother. She carried a small glass, containing a pale green liquid, which she offered to Marcus with a few words that Dinah did not understand.

'Thank you,' he said, and the woman gave Dinah a long, hard stare, said something else and went out of the room.

'If that's for me,' said Dinah, 'what is it?' It looked like a crème de menthe, but she didn't think it was.

'A herbal concoction. Good for shock. Lola can provide a remedy for most things.'

She took it from him, and sniffed—it smelt like thyme. There were other ingredients of course, and she said, 'I think I'm over the shock. I had a very large brandy for it on the plane.'

But bursting into tears just now had shown that she was not as calm as she might be. 'Drink it,' he said. 'It's quite palatable.'

She hesitated, holding the glass, looking at him, undecided whether to say, you drink half and I'll finish it off. Then, with her eyes still on him, she sipped.

It was like cough mixture from her childhood, and she gulped down the rest. He said, 'Good girl. Half an hour, then.'

'Thanks for the witch's brew.'

'You're right there. Now she's fetching something for the bruising.'

'But I don't have any bruises. Well, none I've noticed.' He indicated a mirror, and she looked at her tear-stained reflection, with her mascara rubbed into dark blotches on her cheeks. She shrieked, 'I look *terrible*! Do tell her it's smudged make-up.'

'You have your bath and she'll leave the stuff here. When she sees an instant cure, it will make her day.'

'All right,' she said, and went into the bathroom, smiling.

Thalia's bathroom could have been a film star's, it was so opulent, and Dinah poured the lotion from the bottle that looked prettiest and smelt nicest into the sunken bath with its golden dolphin fittings, and decided she had not been drugged.

Even allowing for the relaxing effect of a fairly leisurely bath, she was feeling much better. She had no bruises. She examined herself in a wall of mirrors, mopping away the steamy haze with a towel, and she had nothing to show for her accident. Except, of course, a caseful of ruined clothes and a wrecked car at home. Some of her clothes might be salvaged, perhaps Lola had a miracle mix that made oil and grease vanish, but right now it was either back into her crumpled dress or borrowing something from what looked like enough to stock an average boutique.

And these were all in a villa they only used occasionally. Spread over other homes, Thalia must have mountains of clothes, so she could certainly spare one garment for a few hours.

It was a temptation to select a knock-out. The colours were glorious and striking, and the material made her feel like purring: satin, fine lawn and lovely, lovely silk.

It would have been fun to try them on, and if she had been in here for the night she might have had her own fashion show, but her half-hour was nearly up. She took down one of the less flashy numbers, a caftan that Thalia might be less likely to complain was her favourite model.

From the cosmetics, she helped herself to a moisturiser that would have been way out of her usual price range. She had lipstick in her purse in the other room, she could get that later. Now she didn't look too bad— she was unbruised, unmarked. Then she picked up the little earthenware pot that was out of place among the silver-topped, cut-glass containers.

This had to be 'something for the bruising', it was smooth and pale as cream, but the smell wrinkled her nose. She was glad she didn't really need this, and she dabbed a tiny smear on her cheeks.

She was past the half-hour now. Out in the courtyard, or somewhere near, Marcus Christophi was waiting for her, which should be incredible. When she had stumbled on the clifftop and he had caught her, she had been scared, yet just now in his arms all her tension had drained away. He was the same man, she was the same woman, but there had been no antagonism at all.

And now she was quite happy at the idea of spending the evening with him. She would probably have been happier if Nic had been here, but Nic would come tomorrow, and tonight held no fears for her now. The next few hours could be interesting. Lola's witch's brew was good stuff, clearing her mind and reviving her body. Maybe the day had not been so bad, after all. Her car was insured and she had come out of the crash without a scratch, and the thing she would have chosen to save in her luggage was her camera, which seemed OK.

It could have been worse. She had seen Marcus in a different light. Maybe Thalia would have changed for the better, too. Maybe when she arrived tomorrow and heard the story, she would say, 'What dress would you like to borrow today?'

Dinah grinned at her reflection in Thalia's caftan and thought, if she does, I'll know I'm dreaming or drugged, because Thalia would never say that in a million years! What Thalia is going to say is, don't touch my things!

She opened the doorway, looked out into the courtyard and saw Marcus. He was sitting on a white stone bench, and as he got up and came towards her she could feel Lola's ointment burning on her cheekbones. It must be powerful, and she was glad she hadn't needed a liberal application.

She said, 'I borrowed this, I hope she won't mind. I hope some of my things will be all right. The bruises washed off. I may look washed out, but I'm uninjured.' She was babbling again, and when he reached her the flush on her cheekbones spread, warm and glowing.

'You look beautiful,' he said, and she knew that it wasn't the ointment, she was blushing.

She said, 'Thank you, the medicine worked, too.'

'It usually does.' He put a hand under her arm again, and she felt his touch run through her like a light set to a running fuse.

'Where are you taking me?'

'Where the food is.'

She should be hungry, although she couldn't have swallowed anything right now, because of this tightness in her throat as she walked along beside him. She confessed, 'I had my doubts about that drink. If you'd left me alone with it, I'd have poured it away. It crossed my mind that somebody might be drugging me.'

'*Drugging* you?' An eyebrow raised. 'What the hell for?'

'I haven't a clue.' She was laughing, and so was he. 'I think I got the wrong idea,' she said.

'So did I.'

So he had changed his mind about her too, and she wondered why, and started to ask, 'What made——' when they came out of the passage through another archway. Mountains rose at the back of the villa, and here a balcony overlooked a lake. Around it, lights burned like torches, and the water looked still and dark and deep.

She had never seen such brilliant stars, and she went to the balustrade, resting her hands on it. It was heart-stopping, stepping out into a night like this. The view from the cockpit over the Cornish coastline had been splendid, but this had the grandeur of a vast isolation. It was awesome, she was almost afraid to speak. She looked for a long time, and then lifted her eyes to the face of the silent man beside her.

He was the right one to be here with. He seemed part of all this, and she heard herself ask, 'Were you born here?'

'I was born in England. Why?'

'Just that——' it wasn't easy to explain '—the setting seems right for you.'

'My father was born in this house. So was Nic's. We spent most of our holidays here as children—it was always our second home. Won't you sit down?'

There were two chairs at a table that was laid with a dozen different dishes. From Greek restaurants at home she recognised the stuffed vine leaves, the salad topped with black olives, and Lola was carrying in a soup tureen.

As she began to serve, she stopped and stared. Dinah was sitting in shadow, but her skin was glowingly unblemished, and for a moment Lola could not believe it. Then she smiled and said, 'Very good.'

'Splendid,' said Marc. 'Miss Marsden is very grateful.'

'Thank you,' said Dinah, because the herbal tonic had certainly worked. Before it, she had felt like a wet rag, now she felt wonderful.

Lola finished dishing the soup: chicken, eggs, rice and the tang of lemon. It was delicious. Dinah was suddenly ravenously hungry, making quick work of it, when she realised that Marcus was leaning towards her with a wry expression.

Spoon poised, she stared at him and he asked, 'Did you put some of that stuff on?'

'Only a touch on my cheeks.' She hadn't cared for the smell herself. 'Is it that pungent?'

'It's beating the garlic.' He took a napkin and dipped it in a silver finger-bowl in which yellow petals floated, then cupped her chin in his hands and wiped her cheeks gently.

There was such comfort in him. He could make her feel as cherished as a child with a smudge on her nose. She said, 'I thought if she didn't smell it, she might smell a rat!'

'That was thoughtful of you.'

He poured a pale rosé wine into two goblets, and she asked, 'Does it work?'

'Not quite that fast, but it's effective. I was smothered in it more than once when I was young. The smell never seems to change. As I got older, my skin got more leathery, thank God.'

'You don't bruise now?'

'I don't fall now.'

'I wonder you don't patent the formula. There must be a market out there for that green tonic, too. That was an instant reviver. Good for the appetite, too!' And she finished her soup to prove it.

'I don't think it would travel,' he told her gravely. 'Everything grows around here, and has to be picked by the light of a full moon like tonight.'

'You're joking, aren't you?'

'Not entirely.'

This time, Ireni appeared, to remove the soup plates and put down grilled red mullet and vegetables and look at Dinah. Lola must have gone back boasting of the speed of her cure. Ireni was impressed and Dinah said, 'Thank you for everything. I'm sorry I left you with that mess in my case.'

'I do my best,' said Ireni, which didn't sound too hopeful, and Dinah said,

'Thank you' again. When Ireni vanished, she asked, 'Did Lola have anything for Nic's injuries?'

'She mixes him draughts, but he doesn't drink them often.'

'He is all right, isn't he?'

'Yes.' He qualified that with, 'The breaks are taking their time, and he still gets the occasional headache.' Immediately, she was alarmed.

'Headaches? Is that why he's seeing a doctor?'

'Routine. There's nothing to worry about.'

She was reassured that she was being told the truth. Nic had not quite recovered, but he would. He was convalescing, and all would be well. 'And I owe you an apology,' said Marcus.

That made her smile. 'He's remembered he asked me to marry him?'

They had both been suspicious about that. When Nic confirmed it, both Marcus and Thalia would owe her an apology, but Marcus said, 'No, but that's no matter. He wants to marry you.'

'And that's enough?'

'It's enough for Nic.' He looked steadily into her puzzled eyes. 'It's enough for me.'

'What changed your ideas?'

'The day I left England, there was a phone call to the house. A Samantha Smith and a Steve Wilson.' She waited, the names meant nothing to her. Then she had it, they were on the clifftop when Nic fell.

'Of course! I'm glad they rang, they were marvellous. She gave me a phone number, only I lost it. I hoped they read in the papers that Nic wasn't badly hurt.'

'He said you went over the cliff after Nic.'

'So?'

'That you didn't stop at all, you just went after him.'

She made a self-mocking grimace. 'Sometimes I'm not very bright, but I'm very agile.'

He smiled. 'And they were wondering about you, because you looked awful, and anybody could see you were worried to death.'

'Well, I was.'

'So you care about him,' said Marcus, 'and I had no right to suggest otherwise. And while you are here, could we call a truce?'

'Yes, please.' She made a joke of it. 'You're not doing a U-turn far enough to give us your blessing?'

'I told you, I'm not his guardian. He doesn't need my blessing.'

'I think he does. Your approval, anyway. Are you saying you suddenly don't mind us getting married?'

'Being here together for a while, you might have second thoughts. If not, then if you want my blessing you can have it. You haven't known each other very long.' He helped himself to several of the side dishes. Till now they had sat with the main course cooling on their plates, but now they began to eat.

'You did mean me to come.' She had been almost sure of that before, but now she was certain. 'So why did you more or less order me to keep away?'

'I felt the invitation should come from Nic,' he said solemnly, but he didn't expect her to believe that.

'And from you it would have seemed like an order.' She sounded rueful because she had reacted exactly as he thought she would, admitting, 'You're right. I wouldn't have come. I can't stand big, bossy men.'

He considered that, then asked, 'Is it being given orders that bothers you, or big men?'

'The two together. Nobody likes being pushed around, but when big men start shoving I really dig my heels in.' She looked into the tough, arrogant face that was smiling at her. 'Some men seem built for aggro.'

'Are you referring to my weight or my nose?'

Perhaps she was getting too personal. He looked hard-muscled, not overweight. She had been in his arms twice, and it had not been a cushioning closeness. She gulped and quipped, 'Well, the first time I saw you, I thought you looked like a heavyweight boxer.'

'I did get it in a fight, but not a professional one.'

'Who won? Don't tell me. I'm a peaceful girl myself.' You won, she thought, you'd always win.

'Unless big men order you around?'

'Well, yes.'

'I'll remember that!' And they were both laughing.

Afterwards, they ate their meal and drank their wine, and she told him about the pictures she hoped to take while she was here. 'I've got a friend who runs a picture library. She can always use attractive scenes for travel brochures. Really, I should find plenty to photograph, shouldn't I?'

After two and a half glasses of wine she could say with mock mournfulness, 'Pity about the nose. Beautiful people in exotic backgrounds always sell well, and your family have such beautiful noses.'

'Mine was never that good. I was never one of the beautiful people.'

'Nic is, isn't he? And Thalia. I'm sure Nic will let me photograph him, but I don't think Thalia will.'

Marcus agreed. 'You may have to settle for Nic and the scenery. Do you ride?'

'Not well.' Occasionally, she had been on horseback, jogging round meadows and along country lanes, but she did not fancy covering this kind of terrain perched on the saddle of a horse.

'Do you swim?'

She loved swimming, she was a strong swimmer. 'Yes, if I've got a swimsuit that isn't ruined.' Or if Thalia cared to lend her something. She looked out over the lake. 'Is that all right for swimming?'

'It's very deep. Have you done any skindiving?'

'Yes, I've done some underwater photography,' she said eagerly.

'Then tomorrow I'll show you the caves.'

Moonlight and stars glittered on the dark water, and she whispered, 'Down there?'

'Yes.'

She had just taken a plump, juicy grape out of a bowl of cold water. She popped it into her mouth now and began, 'What kind of caves?' and found herself stifling a yawn.

'Tomorrow,' he said. 'It's been a long day for you.'

'It got better.' But suddenly it was hard to keep her eyes open.

As he stood up, he asked, 'What was the name of the garage that collected your car?'

'I've got a card in my handbag.'

'Give it to me tomorrow, and I'll find out what's happened.' She pushed back her chair, leaving the rest of the wine and a half-eaten peach on her plate. If she had been less tired, she would have finished both, but she was yawning again, so she let him lead her off the balcony and said, 'Thank you,' because of course she wanted to know about her car.

Lights were on in the courtyard, but there was no sign of anyone. The only sound was the clicking of crickets. Even the fountain was still as Marcus opened her door. She stepped in and he said 'Goodnight.' She called goodnight after him, and when he hesitated and turned a pulse leapt in her throat. He said, 'Sleep late tomorrow. You look all in.'

For a moment, she had actually thought he might walk back and kiss her, or even come into her room. Only for a moment, less time than it took for her to laugh and say, 'Is that an order?'

'I wouldn't dare,' he said, and she went on laughing until she closed the door. Then the laughter stopped, and she crossed to the dressing-table and slumped on to a stool. Her legs were rubbery and her heart was thumping. It *had* been a long day. Fatigue and wine had finally addled her brain, making her imagine a mag-

netism between herself and Marcus inexorably drawing
them together.

She did *not* fancy him. Heaven forbid! In no way was
he her type. Although, sitting here in Thalia's caftan,
she envied Thalia and Nic his strength and his protection.

One of her own nightshirts lay on the bed, so smooth
that it must have been washed and ironed. When she
opened the wardrobe, a few clothes hung there. In a
drawer were some undies, the dressing-table held what
had been salvaged of make-up and toilet requisites, and
a crumpled, paperback novel, a small, sticky address
book and a pack containing the photographs she had
taken in Cornwall. She had been pleased with them, but
now they had absorbed enough hair conditioner to glue
them together.

Ireni must have worked hard and fast while Dinah
was eating her dinner, and here were the bare necessities
to get her through tomorrow at least. Beyond that,
someone would provide. Marcus would arrange it, and
she opened her purse and found the garage card. If
anyone could put her little car together, she thought, he
would. He was a man to make things right for his own
and, if she and Nic decided in the next few weeks that
they wanted to spend the rest of their lives together, she
might be drawn into that circle and no longer the outsider. Tonight, with Marcus on her side, everything
seemed possible.

She slept soundly. No sooner had she fallen into bed
than she went spiralling down into darkness, and the
next thing she knew it was morning.

She lay for a few moments, coming slowly to life.
Usually she snapped wide awake as soon as her eyes
opened, but this morning she could take it easy and she
yawned and stretched, wriggling happily.

Lovely things would be happening today. Nic would be here, and Marcus was no longer hell-bent on parting them. It had been sudden, and it must have been a shock when she announced that Nic had asked her to marry him, bearing in mind his first marriage to Carolyn the gold-digger. A testing time was reasonable, because they should know each other better before they committed themselves.

She had not given Nic her answer when Samantha and Steve had interrupted them, and if there had been no accident she would have said, let's wait until we're sure. We've never been alone together. We don't really know each other.

But now she couldn't wait to see him. She slid out of the silken sheets and stretched again, this time flinging her arms wide and her head back, stiffening as a nerve jabbed. She had slept heavily, lying awkwardly, and now she had a crick in the neck. She rubbed the tender spot, making her way to the bathroom, and under the shower it eased. However, she was still conscious of it as she dressed and, sitting before the dressing-table, she avoided turning her head as she peeled the tacky set of prints apart.

They were all stained and spoilt. She could make out what they had been: the shots in the house, moonlight from the cockpit, Nic in his studio. When she got home, she could soon develop another set. She would have liked to show them to Nic before then, but it was a small thing, and she turned to what was left of her make-up.

That was limited to a mascara wand, a couple of lipsticks and a tube of moisturiser. The rest must have smashed or squashed, and through the windows the sky was blazing blue. She would need to borrow something or get badly sunburned, but she could risk it for a little while.

She applied moisturiser liberally, as far as she could; her stiff neck did not help. Then a touch of coral on her lips, and a flick of mascara. This one was supposed to be waterproof; if she went swimming she didn't want the 'bruises' reappearing! She combed her hair so that it swung smooth and shining. Before Nic came, she would make another foray on Thalia's cosmetics, but this was the best she could do for now, and she stepped out of her room into the courtyard.

The fountain was playing again, and Ireni was sweeping and singing to herself what sounded like a mournful dirge, although she beamed broadly when Dinah called, 'Good morning.'

She came over smiling, enquiring, 'You slept good?'

'Yes, thank you.'

'No bruises.' Ireni tapped her own face.

'None. I'm fine now.' Dinah was not mentioning her stiff neck.

'I will get you breakfast.'

'No hurry, but I would like a drink. Perhaps some fruit juice?' It was a hot day, she had drunk a fair amount of wine last night, and she was parched, longing for a cold drink and then perhaps a cool swim; and she went along to the balcony overlooking the lake, where last night's meal had been served.

By day, the mountains seemed even higher, dotted here and there with a few houses and the pinkish dome of a mosque. A ribbon of road wound upwards, vanishing into what looked like a wilderness of stone and scrub and, incredibly, capping the highest peaks, the whiteness of snow.

Down below, the lake glittered blue-green, with steps leading from the balcony to rockshelf and shingle, against which the water lapped. Ireni had brought a tray laden with food, putting it on the white wrought-iron

table, and Dinah thanked her and filled a glass from the
jug of iced orange juice.

She drank thirstily, looking down from the balustrade. The lake below seemed clear as crystal. She could
see a pattern of rocks and plants, and indigo patches of
deeper water. It was all irresistibly tempting.

She wore a bikini beneath a cotton sundress, and rope
sandals were tied round the ankles. The surface of the
water was almost without a ripple. When she leaned over
from the rock ledge, she half expected to see a reflection
of her own face, and her bright hair did give a glint of
gold to the blue-green water.

It was hard to judge whether it was deep enough here
to risk a dive so she played safe, slipping in feet first,
not touching the bottom, and kicking off into a crawl.
The water looked like a warm bath, but after the sun on
her skin it felt freezing for the first few minutes. She
swam vigorously and then she turned on to her back and
saw Marcus on the balcony.

'Hi, there!' she called. 'It's lovely, but cold.' She
watched him coming down the steps, and swam towards
the ledge, warming up with every stroke. She was pulling
herself out without his help, for he was not offering.
They reached the ledge more or less together, when the
crick in her neck struck again and she landed in a heap,
rubbing it and explaining, 'I've got a stiff neck.'

'Then what are you doing in the water?'

'I forgot it, and I suppose the cold numbed it, but
now it's come back. I must have been sleeping awkwardly last night. I was shattered.' She moved head and
shoulders gingerly, wincing.

'Probably whiplash from yesterday.'

She had been jerked forwards and backwards in her
seat-belt. Without one, she could have smashed through
the windscreen, but the jolt had still been a boneshaker,

and it was a likely explanation. 'It usually takes a while to come out,' he said, 'but if it's only a slight stiffness it should soon wear off.'

That was all it was. She said, 'Promise you won't tell Lola,' and he laughed.

'After her success with the bruises, she'd be delighted to mix you something. You'll be her prize patient.'

'But how would it smell?'

'I can't guarantee roses.'

She joked, '*I* guarantee that, if you tell Lola and I have to rub in any more of her ointment, I'll stay to windward of you all day.'

The sun was so hot, it was already drying her skin. Her pale tan looked anaemic compared with the mahogany darkness of his, but after a week or two here she would be beautifully brown. She suddenly longed to be beautiful, and she found herself wondering what kind of woman Marcus chose.

'Why don't you concentrate on your own love-life?' she had demanded, and he had said 'I give it a great deal of attention.' His women would be glamorous, that was for sure, or was there one special lady?

'You're going to burn unless you put something on,' he said.

This morning she could look after herself, and she had been about to reach for her dress and drape it around her shoulders, but now she said, 'I know, I know,' lifting her dripping hair out of her eyes, taking her time.

'You shouldn't be out here without protective oil.'

'You are.' That was a stupid thing to say, and she went on quickly, 'All I've got left is a tube of face cream. Not sun cream, just face cream, English-climate style. The rest—and, believe me, I came prepared—was that goo in my case.'

'There's plenty around the villa.' Thalia's, of course. Thalia would need to protect her peachy complexion. Nic, too, had a Nordic skin. It was only Marcus who could stroll around, gypsy-dark and impervious.

Guests would have a pleasant time, rubbing in suntan oil and turning bronze, or having the oil massaged in for them. She found herself looking at his hands and she might have asked whether he had many thin-skinned females staying here? However, he spoke first. 'And while you're up there, get a hat.'

She was not trotting anywhere on his say so. 'I'll do that,' she said, 'but first I'll take another dip. I suppose it is safe, swimming here? Nothing comes out of the caves?'

'Not for a very long time.' He didn't advise her against it. If he had done, she probably wouldn't have listened. She went into the water again in a neat, shallow dive, coming up into sunshine gleaming like a sea creature.

If Marcus was watching, he would have seen her performing a stylish repertoire of swimming strokes. She was showing off, and she should be ashamed of her bad manners, when he was only being a considerate host. When she came out, she would say that yes, please, she would like some suntan oil.

But, when she looked across, the ledge was empty. He had not waited to see her swim or sink, and why should he? It was time she was out of the water. A whiplash jerk was an injury, minor in her case, but probably needing rest, not exercise. She could feel the stiffness in her shoulders as she swam back, heading for a strip of shingle, walking up the slight gradient to the ledge beneath the balcony, rather than hauling herself out.

On the ledge, she pulled her dress over her head. It stuck to her, but it was mopping up the wet, then she fastened the laces of her rope-soled sandals round her ankles and climbed the steps to the balcony, using the handrail.

Marcus was sitting there. There was a big, white, fluffy towel on a chair, and she wrapped it around herself and said, 'Thank you.'

'You must have been a stubborn child.' He was laughing at her again, but with the kind of smile that made her smile back. 'Your father must have had trouble with you.'

She had been unreasonable and she wanted to make amends, while emphasising that childhood was long behind her. She said, 'It was the other way round, I had trouble with him,' and she sat down, rubbing her hair with the corner of the towel.

'What kind of trouble?'

He sounded amused, but he could be wondering if a scandal had escaped his investigators, so she said, 'He was a good man in every way. I miss him all the time. But he was a soft touch, I was the one who had to look out for both of us.'

The breakfast tray was still there, and now there was a pot of coffee, too. He poured and handed a cup to her, and she took it carefully, because she did not want her fingers to brush his. She didn't know why, it was an instinctive reaction. 'Everyone spoke highly of him,' he said.

She spooned in sugar—she was going to need energy today—and stirred slowly. Then she said lightly, 'Oh, yes, you had me investigated, didn't you? What did everyone say about me?'

'Your colleagues and neighbours like you. A nice girl, they said, and smart.'

'That's nice.' She took a good gulp of coffee, and looked at him, half in earnest as she said, 'I wish I could afford to have you investigated.'

'Why me? Nic's the one you're concerned with.'

'I think your dossier would be better value for money.' She added gaily, 'And worth a fortune.'

He was smiling, too. 'You wouldn't be talking blackmail?'

'Actually, I was talking rubbish. How did you go about it?'

'A few questions here and there.'

Even in this heat, it was a chilling thought, and suddenly she was resentful. She took a croissant, buttered it and topped it with apricot conserve, and said, 'I could have filled in a questionnaire and saved you the trouble. I don't have any secrets.'

'Did that happen when you went down the cliff-face after Nic?'

'What? Oh, that.' She looked at her sprawled legs, long and slim and lightly tanned, except for the pink knees. A fortnight had healed scratches and grazes, but the marks were still there.

She nodded and he said ruefully, 'We both seem to have this protective streak. You looked out for your father, and I can't stop believing I'm responsible for my two.' The admission disarmed her, and he went on, 'They were so young when the plane crashed, a couple of children. Over ten years was a big enough gap to make me a father figure. That was what they needed at the time, and old habits die hard.'

'Don't they just?' In Cornwall, she had believed that she and Marcus had nothing in common, but it seemed they had a great deal. She had never found it hard to talk to people, but although people had often told her their troubles she rarely responded with her own. Now she found herself confiding in him. 'I got into the habit of disliking big men who give me orders when I was— oh, about ten, I should think.'

'Tell me.'

'It's not very exciting, but it's true. There was this businessman, and my father had some property he wanted. This man was very big—well, he seemed big to me, and he bullied my father, who hated any sort of unpleasantness. I suppose it was after that that I took over, from watching he wasn't shortchanged in shops, to stopping him investing in harebrained schemes. He was a dreamer.'

'Wasn't it a hard life for a small girl?'

'Oh, *no.*' She leaned forwards, eyes shining. 'I had a super life as a child. I've always had a super life. I lost my mother a long time ago, but my father loved me very much, and I guess I was born bossy because I liked watching out for him. And he cared for me. He was always there when I needed him. He taught me all the tricks of the trade in my work.'

Her voice trailed into silence. Her loss was still recent enough for grief to pierce her, and she blinked fast. It would have been dreadful if she burst into tears again, although when he said, 'He must have been very proud of you,' she had to gulp down a sob.

She said, 'I was proud of him.'

'I'm sure you were.' She felt his understanding and support as tangibly as if he had reached across and taken her hands in his. When he said, 'How did the pictures you took in Cornwall turn out?' she knew that it was to cheer her up.

'Not badly. Only the proofs were in my case, and now they're scented and sticky.'

'May I see them?'

'Surely.' She got up, her wet dress clinging to her. 'I'll shower and change and borrow some of Thalia's sun cream. When do you think they'll be back?'

'Some time this evening. We'll go down to the harbour and meet them. If we take it easy, we can spend the day getting there.'

She wasted no more time. She hurried back to her room and collected bra and pants and another dress from her limited wardrobe. In Thalia's bathroom, she washed her hair and applied sun cream, massaging the back of her neck and counting her blessings, because she was lucky to be alive and young on a marvellous day like today.

Then she helped herself to anything she fancied on the dressing-table, applying make-up with a light touch and getting a pleasing result. Before long, the heat and the dust would take over, but she would start off looking good.

As she stepped into the courtyard, she saw Marcus through an open doorway in a room that was obviously an office. He was watching her. He came out, closing the door behind him, asking, 'Ready?'

'Yes.' She almost ran to him and said gaily. 'I'm protected against the sun, I'm covered in sun cream and I've got a scarf I can wear on my head. Anything else you're going to warn me against?'

'Would I be likely to warn you, and lose the advantage of surprise?' His grin was wicked and warming, and she laughed, throwing back her head, feeling the sun on her face.

He was joking, of course. But it meant that she looked fetching, and maybe that was what she had been aiming for. Admiration from Marcus.

Rubbish, she told herself. I want him as a friend, I don't want him to fancy me. And then, as he took her arm and again that dizzying rush of sensation went through her, she knew that if he ever did, even for a little while, she could be in real danger.

CHAPTER FIVE

THERE was a Range Rover on the helicopter pad when they came out of the villa, and Dinah joked, 'Not the horses, nor the helicopter?'

'The helicopter's in Heraklion. Would you prefer horses?'

'No, thanks. Not even a mule. Where do you keep the horses?'

'On a farm a few miles away.'

They would have to be hardy animals, and sure-footed. She took her seat, camera bag at her feet, and, reminded of her own smashed-up car, dived into her handbag to find the garage card, the number of her own insurance company and details of the driver who had run into her, taken down rather shakily on the back of a shopping list.

'I don't think there's much hope for it,' she said, 'but I would be grateful if you'd make enquiries. It was a dear little car. I felt rotten abandoning it.'

'Any message?' he said.

'You can laugh. We've been through a lot together, me and my Mini.' She had bought it second-hand, it had been a bargain and she would miss it, but her dancing eyes belied her mournful expression. 'Have you and this one been through a lot together?'

'Put it this way, I wouldn't be sending it get-well cards. You enjoy driving?'

'Very much.' As the car moved on to a road that was a winding, rutted track, she watched him handling the controls, getting them along at a good, steady speed, dodging the bumps.

'You can take the wheel later,' he remarked.

'Can I?' Not in the mountains, but on flatter ground, she would like that, and she asked, 'Do you pilot the helicopter?'

'You want flying lessons?'

'I didn't mean that. I just wondered.'

'I could teach you to fly.' He was probably joking again.

She smiled. 'Is that a promise?'

'Why not?'

'Watch it,' she said gaily, 'promises can come home to roost.' She looked out at the mountain gorge that rose bare and scorched above the zigzagging track, rocks carved by the elements into weird shapes, strange shadows and gnarled trees, and thought, you could teach me. And she was shaken at the way her thoughts ran from there to what she might learn from a man like Marcus Christophi.

The sun was beating down. She tied the scarf around her head, knotting it under her hair in the nape of her neck, and dug into her gadget bag for her camera. She told him, 'I've got one film in here, the rest were in my case; and I'm not too sure about this, either.'

'This' was a pocket recorder that she used as a notebook for anything of interest about her photographs. She pushed the record button and recited a nursery rhyme: 'Mary had a little lamb'. Then she held it towards him like a reporter. 'Would you care to say a few words, sir? Could I interview you on the highspots of this journey?' The tinkling sound of bells reached her and she listened, 'What's that?'

'It could be Pan. This is pagan country.'

Something stirred among the towering peaks, and she said, 'Pan is half-goat, isn't he?'

'So they say, but that's all sheep, and the little hut up there,' which looked like a tiny box, 'is a shepherd's summer-hut.'

'Can I get a picture?' He stopped the car while she changed the camera lens and fiddled and snapped. Then she rewound the recorder, and her voice chirped back at her; so, the shake-up had done it no harm.

She was a tourist that day, a sightseer, delighting in everything. They passed a deserted hamlet of four houses, where doors swung on broken hinges, and a splintering wooden footbridge ran over the dry bed of a mountain stream.

Marcus had known the family who had lived there. The old ones had died and the young ones had moved away, but he told her about old Georgio and his brothers, who were doughty guerrilla fighters in their day, and she took a photograph of a bougainvillaea growing over a tumbled wall. A little while later they stopped again, at a small, white chapel with a faded icon on the wall of a dark-eyed madonna and child, surrounded by gaunt staring saints.

He had known this island and its people all his life. She took pictures and turned on her recorder for his anecdotes and information, and it was all fascinating. But it was also hot, with no breath of wind, and when they reached a village and he said, 'We'll eat here,' she was more than ready to rest in the shade.

Motorcyclists buzzed through narrow streets, and there were tourists here, conspicuous in holiday clothes against the women in black who sat, spinning, knitting, lace-making, in front of the white houses, and the men who sat together, inside and outside the coffee shops, were drinking coffee from tiny cups, or ouzo from small glasses.

As she walked along a cobbled street, and then down the main road, with Marcus, he was hailed by those who seemed to know him well. They waved and called, and he answered. Dinah couldn't understand a word, but from his tone she gathered he was exchanging greetings. Affable and brief. As though he was alone, although she was close by and obviously with him.

The holidaymakers knew she was with him. When they sat down under a pepper tree in the little square, and were served with cold lager and an excellent fish soup, every time she looked around, some woman's eyes were on Marcus. They didn't know he was rich and powerful but, even in a sweat-stained, open-necked shirt, his physique made him impressive. His broken nose gave him a rakish air, and he had a tremendous charisma of strength and sensuality.

Women looked at Dinah as if they would like to be in her place, and he had to be aware of it. It must happen to him all the time in any company, and she frowned slightly, putting down her glass with a little thump.

'What's the matter?' he asked.

'Nothing. Not a thing. I was just thinking I could get a cotton dress here.' Several of the shops around the square displayed clothes of the cheap and cheerful kind, but what she had been thinking was how tough it would be on a girl who really cared for this man. The competition would be constant and killing.

Dinah was not aspiring to anything more than friendship, but she was irritated, and she took an ineffective swipe at a gnat that had just settled on her arm.

'Insect repellant,' she said, 'that's something else I need. They don't bite you, of course.'

'I told you,' he said. 'Skin like an old boot.'

'Could be all that stuff Lola rubbed on you when you were a child.' Laughing, she put her hand on his arm and said, 'I'm having a smashing time. I'm enjoying myself so much.'

He covered her fingers with his own, holding her to him, smiling. 'And I can't remember a better day.'

Of course, she didn't believe that, but it was good to hear, and she said, 'Years ago, I read a story about a girl who felt that everyone was entitled to one year of happiness in her life. I can't remember why, but she totted up the good times, and mostly they only lasted a few minutes or at most a few hours. But if I was doing that I'd count all of today.'

'So would I,' he said.

His arm was hard beneath her hand, his covering fingers were light over hers, and she looked into his eyes and felt as if she was being drawn into him. She was moving closer, her face almost brushing his, and his eyes were dark.

Then he sat back and so did she, and not a moment too soon, she thought. Another moment and she would have kissed him and, although it wouldn't really have mattered, it would have been a silly thing to do. She said, 'I shall buy a yellow dress. I like yellow.'

'A splendid colour,' he said, as their whitebait was served with great wedges of lemon.

'Tell me about this place,' begged Dinah, and listened and laughed and talked and lost count of time.

He knew when they should move on, so there was no hurry. The dishes kept coming, the eating was slow. Some at other tables sat for hours, some moved off to catch their buses, and she grew used to the sidelong glances of other women. She started to smile at them, meeting their eyes, and then they usually looked away hastily.

One very pretty girl, with a nice-looking boy—they could have been students—who was eyeing Marcus as he talked to a waiter, grinned at Dinah and mouthed, 'Swap?'

The boy was busy comparing menu prices, and Dinah burst out laughing and shook her head. Marcus turned and asked, 'What's the joke?'

'I've been offered an exchange. You, for the lad with a tiger on his T-shirt.'

He laughed. 'You'd be doing her no favours. She'd do better to stick with what she's got.' And the girl pulled a face and grinned again, and leaned over her companion to point out what she wanted on the menu.

A little later, Dinah took photographs of the square and the café cats, with the students in the background, because they were a memory that would always make her smile. Then, putting aside her camera, she brought out the pack of Cornish proofs and opened it up.

They were still tacky. She hadn't bothered cleaning them, because the damage had been done. She would develop another set for Nic, these were for throwing away, but Marcus had asked to see them.

She had to explain some of them. 'This was a moonlight view from the cockpit, and I took this in Nic's studio.'

He was in profile. The background of a Minoan fresco had bubbled and peeled, and Nic's classical features looked like marble. 'Interesting,' said Marcus.

'Before the hair conditioner got at it, this was a good picture.'

'I believe you.'

'But he still looks like a Greek god. They both do.' Thalia's wild hair and sultry beauty would have been quite at home around Olympus.

'They always make a pretty pair,' Marcus agreed. And, when she looked at him thoughtfully, he asked, 'Are you trying to place me in the mythology of my ancestors?'

That was not why she was suddenly serious. It was hearing yet again how close Nic and Thalia had always been. Close as twins, Nic had said, so to Thalia another girl would always be an intruder. The next few weeks would not be easy, but now she went on with the game, suggesting gaily, 'Maybe the Minotaur?'

'Half-man, half-bull.' His voice rumbled deep. 'An ugly mixture. I wonder if there was anyone like you in the maidens who were served up to him each year as tribute.'

'I hope not! She wouldn't have stood much chance if she'd been like me—I can never find my way out of mazes. I'm always the one where a man has to climb up on a ladder and shout directions, and that can be very humiliating. You feel such a fool.'

They were both laughing and she was joking, because usually she knew where she was going. Soon they would be meeting Nic and she said, 'Watch the time. Give me time to do my shopping. I don't want to have to start sponging on Thalia when we get back.'

She bought a yellow sundress, a white cotton blouse with long, loose sleeves, and a full cotton shirt in shades of green, from palest lime to deepest blue-green. The colours of the lake.

She left the shop with her arms full, and Marcus left the man he was talking to and came to meet her. The man watched them. He was bearded, wearing a broad-brimmed black hat, and she wondered if Marcus had told him who she was and, if he had, how he had described her. As Nicholas's friend? Nicholas's fiancée? He had not introduced her to anyone, although the man still stood staring after them.

She said, 'I want a chemist's to get some cream, and I shall need some more films.'

Marcus replied, 'There are more shops by the harbour.'

They drove to the coast through olive groves and vineyards, with the scent of pines drifting in on the hot air. The harbour seemed much bigger from the hillside than it had when she had looked down from the helicopter only yesterday. He parked near the quay and they walked between tiers of houses through narrow, busy streets, stopping to buy what she needed, then coming out to the deep-water harbour.

The boats had looked like toys from the air. There were dinghies bobbing alongside the harbour wall and, farther out, fishing-boats; now there were yachts, motor cruisers, and a pleasureboat. 'There's the *Condor*,' said Marcus, pointing towards a big white boat.

He went to the harbour wall, and on deck a man waved his arms, signalling. 'They're ashore,' Marcus told Dinah. 'We'll look around for them.'

They didn't have far to look, no further than a taverna courtyard a stone's throw away.

An archway and a narrow passage led to it, and Dinah's heart gave a happy skip at her first sight of Nic sitting there, so handsome, relaxed and elegant. There was a bottle between them, and a dish of sweetmeats, from which Thalia was picking. Thalia popped whatever it was she had selected into Nic's mouth, then found another for herself, and as Dinah stepped out of the passageway, with Marcus behind her, it was Thalia who looked round and saw her.

She said something silently, her lips shaped an expletive, and she closed her eyes, as if shutting out the sight might make Dinah vanish.

Seconds later, when Marcus's shadow fell across their table, Nic was pouring wine and Thalia sat with her face still turned away.

'Dinah!' Nic couldn't believe his eyes either, but his delight was as transparent as Thalia's hostility. 'How did

you get here?' He jumped up, reached for her with his left hand—his right wrist was still strapped—and Marcus picked up a chair in each hand, set them at the table and seated himself.

Dinah said, 'I arrived last night. How are you? You were getting a check-up—is everything all right?' Her eyes searched Nic's face anxiously. He looked fit, except for the wrist, and he kissed her warmly.

'Absolutely. Especially now you're here. Why didn't you let us know when you were arriving?'

'I did as soon as I knew.' She sat down beside him. 'I got a cancellation for a morning flight, and I rang your London office as you told me to, and they said they'd get right through to you.'

'The call must have come after we'd left,' said Nic. 'Have a good journey?'

'Yes, thank you,' said Dinah, 'although I wrote my car off on the way to Luton.'

Of course, he wanted to hear about that, but she hadn't been hurt and it was a run-of-the-mill accident, braking suddenly and getting hit from behind. She described it briefly, and was startled when he said, 'You wouldn't have organised that, I suppose, Marcus, to stop Dinah coming?'

Marcus said, 'You get some funny ideas.'

And Dinah gasped, 'What?'

'He's *joking*;' Thalia said witheringly, and of course Nic *was* joking.

He was in high, good spirits, laughing as he said, 'That man is capable of anything. You don't know him.'

But I do, Dinah thought, and then her gaiety faded, because Nic was right. In less than a day, how much could she have learned about a character as complex as Marcus Christophi? He had enough animal magnetism to get under the skin of any red-blooded woman, but he was still a stranger. It was as though a supporting arm had fallen from her, and suddenly it was an effort to keep smiling.

They were all smiling, even Thalia wryly grinning at the absurd suggestion that Dinah's bump had been masterminded. 'Her luggage was in the boot,' said Marcus. 'The case was crushed, and most of the contents. She'll need to borrow some clothes. I'm sure you won't mind.'

'Won't I?' said Thalia.

Dinah said quickly, 'I'll manage, I went shopping this afternoon.'

Nic said, 'Well, you had a lucky escape,' and for the first time since morning she was aware of the slight stiffness in her neck.

'Just a touch of whiplash, and I've had heat therapy on that all day.'

'Come and have it kissed better.' He pulled her towards him, gently massaging the back of her neck, making her giggle with an urge to rub noses, Eskimo fashion, as their faces brushed.

Then Thalia shrieked, and so did Dinah, as half a bottle of red wine slurped into her lap. Thalia grabbed a paper napkin, babbling, 'Oh, clumsy me! Can you mop it up? I can't tell you how sorry I am.'

Don't even try, Dinah thought furiously. Nic was mopping her down as the wine soaked in, and he made sympathetic noises, but he had no suspicion that this had not been an accident. He scolded Thalia cheerfully. 'I can't take you anywhere, you ham-fisted little scruff!'

The widening red stain looked gruesome, and Dinah said, 'There goes another dress.'

'After this, Thalia will be delighted to let you have anything you need,' said Marcus. He knew she had sent that bottle spinning deliberately. His voice was grim, and Dinah got up, holding the stickiness away from her.

'I'll have to get out of this. It looks ghastly.'

Staff were milling around, whisking away the empty bottle, wiping the table, smiling at the 'mishap', and a girl was indicating the door to the kitchens, and somewhere where Dinah could clean up. However, that would still mean walking back to the car in a sopping wet dress.

'Shall I slip out and buy you something?' Thalia suggested sweetly. 'I'd be delighted to lend you something, but I don't have much on under this. Are you wearing anything underneath? Shall we go back to the *Condor*?'

'Put this on,' said Marcus, stripping off his shirt. 'I'll bring the car down. It's time we were leaving. Give me five minutes.'

He didn't really need his shirt, lots of men around were stripped to the waist, and once Dinah reached the car she could put on the dress she had bought today. She thanked him, and took his shirt with her into the primitive washroom.

The rate she was going through clothes, she could finish this holiday in a bikini, although Thalia owed her for this. She had knocked over that wine on purpose, probably aiming for Dinah, although Nic had been lucky. Her idea was to stop the caress and the kiss. Ham-fisted little scruff she was not, jealous little bitch she was, and Dinah would have no qualms in replacing this from her wardrobe.

She swilled the stain on the dress, reducing it to a stubborn pink, swabbed her stomach and legs, and pulled Marcus's shirt over her head. Enveloped in its folds, she found her nostrils filled with the male smell. Sunshine and sweat, earthy and heady. He used an aftershave with a clean, faint tang, she remembered that from last night, but no aftershave lingered on this shirt. And although she had hardly glanced at him when she took it, it evoked a memory of a bronzed, hard body, massive shoulders and dark, curling chest hair.

The smell and the image were not unpleasant, but the fit was ridiculous. It hung on her like a small tent, until she pushed up the sleeves and tied her headscarf round her waist. When she went back, Nic said, 'You'd have looked better in mine, it would almost have fitted, and mine's silk.'

'So it is.' She played fingertips caressingly along his shoulderblades. 'It feels lovely. If this happens again, I shall expect you to strip off.'

Nic grinned, Thalia glared and Dinah thought, I'm getting as bad as she is, but I don't think she'll spill anything else on me.

The car arrived as they came through the archway. 'Good timing,' said Dinah.

'He's known for it,' said Thalia.

Nic opened the back door as it drew up beside them among the holidaymakers. 'In you get, darling.' And he climbed in after Dinah, while Marcus reached to open the passenger door for Thalia.

Nic winced, flopping back in his seat, but smiled in answer to Dinah's alarmed look. 'They're knitting nicely, but I still get the twinges.'

'A shame, when you've come all this way, isn't it?' Thalia turned, peering round the headrest. 'But loverboy isn't going to make the earth move just yet.'

'Oh, shut up,' said Nic.

'Just warning her,' said Thalia. 'And you. We don't want you straining anything that isn't up to it.'

'That's enough!' said Marcus.

'Ignore her,' Nic said to Dinah. 'She always was a cheeky child.'

Dinah had nearly laughed, because that was exactly how Thalia had sounded, but she was more likely to be

trying to shock than amuse, so Dinah kept a straight
face and Thalia began to chatter about the party they
had attended last night. It had been on Rhodes, at the
home of a famous actor and his fourth wife.

She rattled off jet-set names, some of which Dinah
had heard, and the gossip was sharper than any gossip
page—who was with who, and which relationships
looked shaky. 'We left earlyish,' said Thalia. 'Nic was
beginning to feel ragged, and you were missed.' She
meant Marcus. 'They all wanted to know where you
were.'

There were messages for him, mostly from women,
and Dinah, who was not interested in this, said softly
in Nic's ear, 'It must have been quite a party.'

'Not bad,' he said, 'but if I'd known you were on
Styros we wouldn't have been there. You're even prettier
than I remember.'

He sounded as if they had been apart for a long time,
and she said, 'It's nice to know I'm wearing well. I had
a hectic fortnight, working overtime so that I could take
time off.'

'How long can you stay?'

'Two weeks. Maybe three.'

She was whispering to get a little privacy from the two
in the front seats. Although Thalia was talking non-stop
into Marcus's ear, Dinah suspected that he could block
Thalia out if he wanted to hear what she and Nic were
saying.

So she kept her own voice hushed, and Nic followed
suit, asking, 'Did Marcus meet you at Heraklion?'

'No. Somebody met me and took me to a helicopter.
Marcus was at the villa.' She grinned, then pulled a face.
'I'm on trial here. This is your chance to get tired of
me.'

'No danger of that,' said Nic. 'I'm crazy about you. Before you leave, I'm going to put the biggest ring I can lay my hands on on your hand.'

She noticed he was not considering he might be on trial too, or that there was any risk she might be less than crazy about him.

But she pushed that niggle from her mind. With all he had to offer, he was obviously a better prospect than she was. All she could bring to a relationship was herself. He came with spectacular good looks and charm, and also with a glittering life-style that his wife would share. What girl in her right mind would not accept Nicholas Christophi?

She looked up, to meet Marcus's eyes in the driving mirror, and wondered if he could lipread. She had been going to tell Nic that she loved him, but instead she said, 'It's a long ride back.' Marcus was not even looking at her, just checking the road behind, but somehow she could not say, 'I love you, Nic,' facing his cool, analytical gaze.

They made no detours on the return journey, and when Thalia stopped chattering she pressed a switch for music, which blasted out and was promptly turned down by Marcus. Nic and Dinah sat comfortably close, talking a little, smiling at each other. When Nic yawned, she murmured, 'Tired?' and he whispered back, 'Yes. Whatever she says, we didn't leave that party until dawn, and then I had to drag her away. She must have danced with every man there.'

Dinah could imagine Thalia being in demand, no matter how glamorous the company. She could see her dancing and flirting, a born exhibitionist, while Nic watched tolerantly, letting her play on. As he had marched her away in the end, she probably believed they had left early, but no wonder Nic was exhausted now.

'Go to sleep,' Dinah whispered, and she put a gentle arm around him, and smiled to herself, remembering the boy on the cliff-face when she had knelt over Nic, desperately trying to comfort him, although he couldn't hear a word she was saying.

'I wouldn't mind a nanny like you myself,' Steve had said, and here she was being a nanny again. When Nic closed his eyes, she kissed his cheek, and it was tenderness she felt, not passion.

In spite of the bumpy roads, it was relaxing and restful back here. Soon her own eyelids drooped, and a little while after that she heard Thalia say, 'They're both asleep.'

Thalia had turned again in her seat and was watching them; Dinah lay still, tempted to glare but deciding against it.

'Poor old Nic,' said Thalia, and Dinah thought, you're a fine one to talk! Who kept him at last night's party till morning?

'He won't find out I knew she was arriving yesterday, will he?' said Thalia.

'No,' said Marcus.

'What's going to happen?' sighed the girl.

'Don't worry,' said Marcus. 'He'll get over it.' He sounded as if he was smiling.

'Promise?'

'I promise,' said Marcus, and Thalia probably smiled too, yawning again.

'Wake me up when we get there.'

'What time did you leave the party?' said Marcus.

There was no reply from Thalia. The music played on and Thalia curled up, but Dinah was no longer drowsy. She had been jolted out of sleep because she did not believe they had been talking about Nic's physical condition. It was recovery from her they meant, from the sickness of an unsuitable love affair. After that, her mind was wide awake, although she lay still for a long time, only shifting slightly when the back of her neck stiffened and cramp threatened.

Nic slept on and so did Thalia. When the music stopped, their breathing was deep and regular. It was another night of the full moon and a sky full of stars, and she believed now that the mountains were alive and haunted. There was a witchiness in the trees flaring briefly in the headlights, and beyond the breathing of the sleepers and the hum of the engine she could imagine a throbbing like a giant heartbeat.

If she had been on home territory, she might have told Marcus to stop the car, and let her out, but here she was an alien in a strange land, so she lay still and talked to herself inside her head.

Marcus had been weighing her up ever since she had got here. He had used the time they were alone for just that; he had meant them to have time alone. And he was not on her side, he still did not want her in the family. She was a calamity to Thalia, who was open about it, but she had begun to believe that Marcus was unprejudiced.

Well, he was not, and anger burned in her. If Nic had not been sleeping so peacefully, with his head on her shoulder, she would have squirmed out of Marcus's shirt, rolled it into a bundle, tossed it into the front seat and hissed, you can have your stinking shirt back!

She was not staying on here, because there was nothing to be gained. The verdict was fixed; if Nic needed Marcus's approval, there was not a hope in hell. So Nic had to make up his own mind, if he was his own master, and whichever way he decided she was not hanging around to be made a fool of by his family.

Her breath came hard between her teeth, and Marcus said quietly, 'Awake?'

'I haven't been sleeping.'

'You should. It would shorten the journey.'

'Why didn't you tell Nic I was arriving yesterday?'

'Because he was due for a check-up. He might not have gone, and it might have been a mistake. Yesterday's tests were satisfactory, but if he'd known you were arriving he could have turned macho and declared himself fit. You may not have realised how isolated the villa is at times. It isn't always possible even to fly in and out.'

She supposed that made sense. She asked, 'What were you promising he'd get over?'

'The accident, of course.'

'Not me?'

'You don't consider yourself part of the accident?'

She wanted to believe him. She wanted to believe he could be her friend. 'Some do,' she said. 'That's why I got the wine in my lap.'

'I apologise for that.'

'How was it your fault? You didn't throw it.'

She had to smile, and he chuckled too, before replying, 'I'm apologising for not stopping it.'

'Were you expecting it? Does she throw a lot of bottles?' Her voice was normal conversation pitch now, she was not whispering to spare Thalia's blushes. If the wretched girl *did* blush, which Dinah considered unlikely.

'None that I've heard of,' said Marcus.

'But that was deliberate.'

'I'm afraid so.'

'I suppose I should be thankful she didn't hit me over the head with it. Is she asleep?'

'Sound asleep.'

'You thought I was.'

'This one I can vouch for. How's Nic?'

Nic's head had flopped away from her shoulder when she had leaned forwards, but he showed no signs of being disturbed. If he heard or saw anything, it was in untroubled dreams. 'Dead to the world,' she said.

Marcus said, 'They're very alike. You could win Thalia round.'

'You've got to be joking!' This time her voice did rise, but neither sleeper stirred. 'She thinks I've lured Nic away. She hates my guts.'

'Because she doesn't know you. The first we heard of you was after the accident, and the accident was shock enough for her. After Carolyn, Thalia is biased, but if you give her a little time she'll come round, and there will be no more tantrums, no more spilt wine. I'll guarantee her good behaviour.'

What had Dinah to lose? Thalia was spoiled, but she and Nic were very fond of each other, and Thalia could be seeing Dinah as a second Carolyn. She said wryly, 'Could I have the good behaviour bit in writing?'

'You can have my word.'

Sitting behind him, she reached farther forwards, touching his shoulder as she said, 'All right.' Again, briefly, his hand covered hers. A pact in the dark, she thought, and she put her fingers to her lips because they were tingling. 'But when she knows me, she still might not like me. Could she change Nic's mind, too?'

'You're the only one who can do that,' said Marcus. 'You could decide you don't want to marry him, after all.'

'Why not?'

'You might decide to marry me.'

She laughed, because of course that was a joke, and she said, 'Quite a few women at that party seem to have decided they'd like to marry you, going by the messages

Thalia brought back.' And she found she could have repeated all the messages, and the names, although she honestly hadn't thought she was listening.

'All talk,' he said.

'There's a lot of it about. They must have very easy consciences.' Nic and Thalia were sleeping like babies.

'They've always been heavy sleepers. From when they were children they could go out like a light, and once they did they took some waking.'

'Does that run in the family?'

'No.' These two must have felt secure all their lives that somebody was watching out for them. The car took a bump in the road with a little judder and leap, but Nic and Thalia slept on, deeply unconscious.

Marcus said, 'They've slept through force eight gales on the *Condor*, and once through a small earthquake.'

'An earthquake? Where?'

'Here on Styros. Half the house we were staying in fell down while they were sleeping in their beds, covered in dust. We could stop this car now and leave them till morning. When we came back, they'd never know.'

'Never know what?'

'Where the missing hours went.'

'I don't believe you.'

He took the car off the track and it bucked to a standstill. She put out a hand to steady Nic and asked, 'How do we wake them?'

'Shake them. They can't have had much sleep last night. They're making up for it now.'

'We can't shake Nic.'

'No reason why we should. You can shout in his ear when we reach the villa. And if you're sleeping together get him to come to your room. If he dozed off, waiting, you could raise the household before you woke him.'

She should be cool about that, but the idea of her trying to rouse a comatose lover by shaking and shouting, and alerting everybody else but Thalia, was irresistibly comic. Her 'Thank you, I'll try to remember,' was interspersed with laughter.

Marcus opened his door, got out of the car, unfolding his full length, then opened her door. Dinah climbed out gratefully, stretching her legs, then her back and shoulders. A little break in the open air was due. It was a tiring ride, especially for a driver with two snoring sleepers dulling his concentration. The engine was silent now, and Nic on the back seat and Thalia in the front breathed deeply in unison.

I could walk into Nic's bedroom in hobnailed boots, Dinah thought, and he would never hear me. That first night in Cornwall, he stood by my bed and I slept on. He didn't try to wake me, but his nearness didn't disturb me.

Marcus was shirtless in the moonlight, for she was still wearing his shirt, and she could feel the hardness of him against her as if he was holding her, although they stood apart. She thought, I would know if you were near, through sleep, through darkness. She thought, I am not moving away from this car, because I still know the difference between love and lust.

She was attracted to Marcus but she was almost sure that she loved Nic, and if Marcus did try anything on she would make enough noise to wake the dead. 'Coming?' he said.

'Where?'

'Down the road and back. I need to stretch my legs.'

'Can't we walk round the car?'

'The road's rough, but it's easier walking.'

He set off into the darkness, moving out of the headlights, and she called, 'Wait for me,' because she was being absurd.

She reached him in seconds. The track was firmer underfoot than the hillside, and after the confined cabin of the car the night air was refreshing. They walked in silence, his long stride adapting to hers and to the road surface. She had always had the gift of the gab, she talked easily, and since she came here she had told him more about herself than she had ever told anyone, but now she could think of nothing to say.

The road was winding. They soon lost sight of the car, and trees obstructed the glow of the headlamps. She couldn't start babbling about how bright the stars were and how high the mountains, and there didn't seem to be anything else that needed saying right now. She waited for Marcus to break the silence. When he did not, she wondered briefly if he resented her following him.

But then he smiled at her and, suddenly, as she smiled back, there was no need for words. Walking together, she felt an immense contentment, as if the silence between them was a kind of intimacy, and she was sorry when he said, 'We'd better go back.'

As they turned the final bend to the parked car, he said, 'You should have made it a bet,' because Nic was not only awake, he was out of the car and standing in the road.

'Where have you been?' Nic called, and she hurried towards him.

'Just up there. I thought you were asleep.'

'I was, but I rolled on my wrist and it woke me up.' He flinched at the painful memory. 'You've been gone at least half an hour.'

'As long as that?' said Dinah.

Marcus got behind the wheel, and Thalia said sleepily and crossly, 'What's the matter? We're only going home. Do stop wittering!'

She fell asleep again quite soon, but finding Dinah missing seemed to have niggled Nic. He wanted to know, 'What were you talking about?'

When she said, 'Nothing,' he looked irritated.

'I can see how that would pass the time.' Then he smiled. 'Sorry, sweetheart, but I've missed you. I don't want you wandering off now I've got you back again.'

'Not for the next three weeks,' she said gaily, and for the rest of the journey she sat with her hand in Nic's hand.

In the villa, she went to her room, carrying the afternoon's purchases. She showered and washed her hair again and tried on the yellow dress. It was fine, she looked all right. Probably not in the same class as the women at last night's party who had sent messages to Marcus, but all right.

The shirt he had lent her lay in a heap on the bathroom floor, and she would wash it before she handed it back. Her own soiled clothes had been laundered beautifully—service in the villa was very efficient—but she had borrowed this, and she would wash it before she returned it.

For now, she dropped it in a drawer, and the dress that was stained with wine she left soaking. If Thalia sent anything else in Dinah's direction tonight she would get it fielded and bowled back, although Marcus had promised no more tantrums.

'Give her a little time,' he'd said, 'and she will come around.' Maybe, thought Dinah, but highly unlikely.

'Or you could decide you don't want to marry Nic, after all,' Marcus had said. 'You might decide to marry me.'

They both knew he didn't mean that, but recalling it took her breath away, because it was an odd thing to say. Or was it? She had heard it before, both from those who were joking and those who were not. He was joking, but it did make her wonder how it could be to belong to Marcus Christophi.

Out in the mountains there had been a rapport between them, but if he had had the right to hold her in his arms and she had had a right to all of him, how much closer would the closeness have been? What would the lovemaking be like?

She was not a girl for fantasising. She was practical, she had always had to be, but she gasped now as a knot of tension in the pit of her stomach relaxed, and rising, rippling waves of sensation suffused her whole body. It was easy to imagine herself receptive and willing. Not hard to imagine a weight upon her that could lift her higher than the mountain.

But it was dumb thinking and dangerous, and she must stop it at once. She sat on the bed, smoothing down her still-damp hair with shaking hands, and when she joined Nic and Thalia in a big room where a long table, set along a wall, was laid with dishes of food, it was nearly ten minutes before she asked, 'Where's Marcus?'

Thalia had just said, 'Shall we eat?'

She had been sitting in a pool of lamplight, turning the pages of a glossy magazine. Nic and Dinah sat on a two-seater settle and Nic asked, 'How's Barbara?'

He had only met Barbara Coade once, when he first went into the salon with his excuse of wanting his photograph taken, but he knew she was Dinah's partner and in charge of the day-to-day running of the studio.

'Very well,' said Dinah. 'She's minding the shop while I'm here.'

'She knows about us?'

'Of course. She knows I went down to Cornwall with you, and she knows why I'm here.'

'Does she know we're getting married?'

Thalia's eyes were still downcast, but her head had a listening tilt.

'Well, no,' said Dinah. Nobody did. She wasn't a hundred per cent sure of it herself.

'Just as well,' said Nic. 'We'll announce it in our own good time.' And Thalia stood up.

'Shall we eat?'

And it was then that Dinah asked, 'Where's Marcus?'

'Working,' said Thalia. 'Something came through while we were out. Big brother's into a big deal.' She helped herself to a slice of quiche and a spoonful of salad. Nic was hampered by his wrist, and Dinah served him and herself, as he indicated dishes and described their contents.

Idly, she asked, 'What's the big deal?'

'Very hush-hush,' said Nic.

'Don't you know? Aren't you partners?'

'Mainly sleeping,' said Thalia, and grinned faintly at Nic. That was probably a family joke.

'Some bid on a take-over,' said Nic. 'That's his province.' He smiled, he wasn't snubbing her. He wasn't particularly interested himself, and she had only asked for something to say, but it showed again that Marcus was the man in charge.

'Well, I hope it goes his way,' she murmured.

'Things usually do,' remarked Thalia quietly.

Thalia went back to her seat under the lamp, with her plate on a table beside her and the magazine on her knee. She ate slowly, leafing through the journal at the same time. She seemed absorbed in the photographs and articles, and she made no attempt to join in their talk.

Nic and Dinah chatted while they ate about where they would go in the next three weeks and what they would do. Nic turned on music, and after a while Dinah said gently, 'Don't you think you should go to bed?'

He smiled his charming smile. 'Best offer I've had all day!'

'That isn't an offer.' She brushed his hair from his eyes with a light touch. 'It's rest you need.'

'I hate to admit it, but you could be right.'

They stood up. Nic, holding Dinah's hand, said goodnight to Thalia, and she looked up, eyes as blank as if she had forgotten they were there. 'What? Oh, goodnight,' and immediately her head drooped again.

All the family bedrooms seemed to lead off the courtyard. By the fountain, Nic kissed Dinah, warmly and sweetly, and asked, 'Will you come with me?'

'I could roll on that wrist.'

'I'll risk it.'

'I've done you enough damage. It was my fault you were pulling up plants on the edge of the cliff. I'm a big, strong girl, your cracked ribs wouldn't stand me lashing out at them in the night.'

He pretended to cringe and she said goodnight again, her lips nuzzling his cheek for a moment. He watched her go to her room and, as she turned in the doorway, he pulled a mournful face with a resigned shrug.

Nic was not up to a passionate reunion, but a little time alone together would have done him no harm. Just a kiss and a cuddle would have been nice.

She kicked off her shoes, picked up a hairbrush and brushed her hair hard, frowning because he had let her go so easily. Blaming Nic, although she was the one who had walked away. If she had wanted to stay with him, she should not have started raising objections.

Someone tapped on her door, and she crossed the room to answer it, thinking if it's Nic, fine. And then, it won't be Marcus. But somehow it was the tall, broad-shouldered image of Marcus that stayed in her mind, as if she expected to see him framed in her doorway.

Thalia stood there. She glanced at Dinah, then looked beyond her into the room and asked, 'Are you alone?'

'Quite alone,' said Dinah brusquely. 'Who were you wanting?'

'You,' said Thalia. 'I want to talk to you.' She gulped. Dinah saw the constriction in her throat. 'Please,' she said, and turned towards her own room.

Dinah followed, barefoot and wryly amused, because the 'please' was out of character. Then Thalia said, 'Bad luck about your luggage,' sounding almost sympathetic.

'It could have been worse,' said Dinah, thinking, it could have been *me*!

Thalia went to the wardrobes that held her clothes, sliding open doors and offering, 'Take what you want.'

Marcus's surety for her good behaviour seemed to be working. Dinah said gravely, 'That is extremely kind of you.'

'Well, I did spill that wine on purpose.'

'You did?'

'Marcus knew.' She faced Dinah. 'He says you knew.' Dinah's ironic look confirmed that. 'He says you're not like Carolyn.'

He must really have lectured Thalia, because there was no sign of malice and mockery, just a deep sadness as she said, 'She nearly killed Nic.'

So it was the memory of Nic's Carolyn that was hurting Thalia. 'She told him she was pregnant, and he can be such an idiot, because she just laughed about it after he'd married her.'

'How awful!' Dinah breathed.

Thalia said in an almost expressionless voice, 'It was, rather. It was just before my twenty-first birthday. He said, "I've got a surprise for you," and he'd designed this jewellery. He gave it to me, and I thought that was the surprise. Only it wasn't. The surprise was this girl he'd only known a few weeks and I'd never met, and they were married.'

Dinah remembered the photograph, the jewellery, the sullen face that must have been masking unhappiness.

'She never loved him,' Thalia said. 'She just wanted money, and Marcus wouldn't interfere. He turned it over to lawyers and told them to pay her. So you see,' she put a hand over her eyes for a moment, then looked at Dinah, coming back from that other time of heartbreak, 'why I wasn't all that thrilled when you said he'd asked you to marry him, and he couldn't even remember.'

Dinah said, 'I'm not like Carolyn,' because Thalia had paused and she had to say something.

Thalia said raggedly, 'I hope not. Nobody should have to go through that kind of hell twice.' Her eyes were anguished, and with a new insight Dinah knew that she was speaking of her own misery as well as Nic's. It was no sisterly affection that Thalia felt for her cousin. She loved him.

CHAPTER SIX

'So, WHAT do you want?' Thalia started swishing the clothes apart, riffling through the row of hangers. 'You're about my height.'

'Could I borrow this?' Dinah took one at random, which turned out to be a cotton trousers and top in a virulent puce, but her mind was whirling, and she had the impression that they both were going through the motions like amateur actors.

'Come in and take anything,' said Thalia and yawned; but that wasn't quite right either, it was a phoney yawn. 'I'm tired,' she said. 'It was a late night.'

Now Dinah was seeing her dancing the night through, with every man at the party, in a different light. Like her constantly changing boyfriends, it was a ploy to make Nic jealous, so that he would see her as a woman, not as a kid sister. 'I slept most of the journey home,' said Thalia.

'So did Nic,' said Dinah, trying to sound cheerful and casual. 'Marcus said you two once slept through an earthquake.'

Thalia gave a little scream. 'We did! Yes! You never live down a thing like that. We weren't together. We were in separate rooms. But Marcus more or less carried us both out, yawning and fighting.'

She laughed, so that at least was a warm and funny memory. 'Marcus isn't a sound sleeper?' asked Dinah.

'Heavens no! I don't think Marcus ever sleeps. He often works all night.'

'I'll see you in the morning,' said Dinah.

In the courtyard, the fountain was still and the crickets' chorus seemed shriller than ever. She walked barefoot from alcove to alcove, looking at the statues without seeing them, stopping at last in front of the door that led to Marcus's office. He might not be in there; the door fitted well, no light showed around it, and she stood, arms folded and hands clenched, trying to think calmly.

Nic did not know how Thalia felt about him. If he had any idea, he would not be so crassly insensitive, and that meant it was not general knowledge, or somehow or other it would have reached him. To their friends they were 'good mates, close as twins.'

But Marcus would know, and it would suit him to keep all the power and money in the family and under his control. She opened the office door without knocking. She would say, A funny thing just happened to me. Thalia's expression was like looking through my viewfinder, and I saw how she really feels about Nic. That's the only match you want for both of them, isn't it? You've never been on my side for a minute.

An archway led into another room, and it was from there that she heard him speaking. In English, pausing, so that he was either dictating or using the two-way radio, and almost at once she changed her mind about facing him with this tonight.

She might start screeching, she was so incensed at his double dealing. If a showdown was going to be remotely rational, it would have to wait till morning. But then Marcus was in the archway, an eyebrow raised as he came into the room and picked up a sheet of paper from a desk. 'Hello,' he said. 'And what can I do for you?'

Nothing! Nothing he did was for her, and when she drew in her breath, she almost spat, you can stop being a hypocrite, for a start! She was almost surprised to hear herself saying, 'I've just left Thalia. She apologised for spilling the wine, and said I can borrow anything I need.'

'Good,' he said, and she took a silent step backwards, towards the door. 'That's what you came to tell me?'

'Yes.' The room was a well-equipped office, so even from this mountain-top hideaway Marcus Christophi still supervised his empire. He was a busy man, big brother on a big deal, still managing to handle the intruder who was threatening his plans for his family.

As she backed away, he watched her, and she was sure he knew she had not come in here just to say what she had said. 'Good luck with the big deal,' she said.

'What big deal?'

She shrugged. 'Whatever.' And she quickly left the room, closing the door behind her. She ran across the courtyard and locked her own door, congratulating herself on showing some common sense.

You did not square up to a man like Marcus Christophi on his own territory. You might say what you had discovered—Thalia is in love with Nic, isn't she?—but quietly, calmly. You did not shriek, Damn you for pretending to be my friend!

In fact, she and Nic were not committed. In Cornwall, the household staff and the nurse knew that Nic was supposed to have asked her to marry him, but if Marcus asked them to 'forget it' they would, and it had been he who suggested there should be no public announcement because Nic needed a peaceful convalescence.

Since she'd arrived on Styros, she could have been just a casual guest. He had kept her in the background, and he had promised Thalia that Nic would get over it. 'Things go the way Marcus plans them,' Thalia had said, and Dinah wondered just how far Marcus would go to make sure they did.

He was working on it. Even the throwaway quip, 'You might decide to marry me,' could have had a purpose. Did he imagine she was greedy enough to start wondering if she might land the bigger fish? Was he trying to take her away from Nic?

Once he had, he'd dump her fast enough. Nic might be angry, but in Marcus's book a few resentful months were better than another unsuitable marriage. And of course the phone call from Sam and Steve had not changed his mind about her. It had just been a way to disarm her, to make the truce he was suggesting sound reasonable.

The whole thing was falling into place, but the joke was on Marcus. He was going to a lot of trouble, but the punchline was that nobody had bothered to ask if she had said yes. They assumed she had jumped at the chance to marry Nic and money, and some time she might tell them she had not. She might have come to love Nic, she could never forget how she felt kneeling beside him on the cliff-face. But the prospect of fighting Marcus as a way of life would be a mighty obstacle. That was, if Nic still wanted to marry her at the end of the next three weeks.

He was annoyed at being left in the car when she had strolled off with Marcus, so he was a little jealous of Marcus. That could be fanned into a blazing row, unless Dinah was careful.

She *would* be careful. Now she knew that the charm and the kindness were calculated, she would be immune to them. And physically she would remember the Minotaur, half-man, half-bull, and tell herself that she found Marcus repulsive.

Maybe she did. With Lola and her potions around, how did she know she was not being dosed with aphrodisiacs? She hadn't imagined how her body responded to his lightest touch. She had never felt anything like that before, and herbs fresh from the mountainside might do weird things to one's nervous system.

But the women at the party and the girl in the café were not under Lola's spell. And, if love potions worked, Thalia would have tried them on Nic. Maybe Marcus Christophi's sexual charisma was inborn black magic!

Dinah's first impression of him had been right: a dangerous man who was her enemy. She was not swimming into any underwater caves with him, although if she got him by surprise she might cut his aqualung!

She started to laugh hysterically, and had to clap her hand over her mouth to steady herself. Now she knew what it was all about, Thalia would no longer rile her. She was sorry for Thalia, who must be desperately unhappy. She could forgive Thalia a lot, but nothing could excuse Marcus; she despised his sort. How many losers would there have to be so that he could win? Her father had been a loser to the likes of Marcus Christophi, and she got ready for bed with bitter memories crowding in on her...

She had still been at junior school when the construction firm had set its sights on their property in the middle of town. Her mother had not wanted to leave, but her father had been first cajoled and then bullied into signing everything they put in front of him.

Dinah had stood on the stairs with her mother listening to the voices that day, and when they had come out of the room a big man had been grinning and her father had looked old. Her father, the neighbours had said, was always a fool to himself, but when Diana Marsden had died, six months later, they all knew it was because she had a heart condition that could not withstand a killer 'flu bug. Nothing to do with moving house. She

had never been strong, and a smaller property should
have made life easier for her. But Dinah had seen how
she had fretted at losing their home. She blamed the
men who had bullied her father. She didn't blame him.
That was the way he was, and just before her mother
died she said, 'You'll have to look after him. He's more
of a child than you ever were.'

There was a supermarket and a block of flats now on
the site of the old house and garden, and a year ago
Anthony Marsden had slipped away in his sleep. He had
loved his daughter, his work and his friends. A good
man if, sometimes, a rotten judge of character; and he
seemed to have that in common with Nic, who couldn't
recognise a liar and a gold-digger when he met one.

Carolyn had been both, and instead of proposing to
Dinah, whom he'd only just met, he might have done
better if he'd taken Thalia. Same background, same
interests, and she certainly loved him.

So did Dinah, of course. But there were differences
and difficulties that could be surfacing soon, with
Marcus making the most of them. She would not be ma-
nipulated by Marcus Christophi. Tomorrow she would
be a step ahead of him all the way.

With all this on her mind, it was not easy to fall asleep.
For a mad moment, she considered creeping out and
down to the lake. But with her luck Marcus would
surface half-way across or swim beneath and pull her
down. There was the squashed paperback from her battered case, but that was a Victorian murder which did
not appeal right now, and going searching for anything
else to read could be embarrassing if she met him again.

She had locked her door, but she was as much a
prisoner as if a bolt had been shot on the outside, all
because of him, although at this hour she didn't really
want to go wandering around. She wanted to lie here,

and relax and sleep. Today had not been all bad. She should have some good pictures, and she reached for the pocket recorder and flicked the rewind.

Her first shot was the shepherd's hut. It came back vividly into her mind, and then there was her own voice reciting 'Mary had a little lamb,' and 'Would you care to say a few words, sir? Could I interview you on the highspots of this journey?'

She lay back on the pillow, eyes closed, the words conjuring up the scenes. He was putting on a first-class act. He didn't sound bored, although he probably was, saddled with the smalltown girl who had caught Nic's fancy. Listening to the deep, sometimes amused, voice, she wondered how often he had asked himself what the hell Nic saw in her.

Her pride had been badly hurt, and the way she felt now she could almost have married Nic to score over Marcus. But that was a terrible thought, and she was appalled it could even come into her mind. On the recorder, Marcus was telling her about Georgio and his brothers, while she was taking the pictures of the bougainvillaea, and she heard herself mutter, 'I think I hate you.' Hate was stronger in her tonight than love. Marcus was blotting out Nic. And she switched off the recorder, because she could not bear to listen to him any longer.

She woke with temples pounding and the sensation of a heavy weight on top of her head. When she did manage to struggle up from the pillow, she sat with her head bowed in her hands for a few minutes more before she could crawl out of bed. Splashing her face with water helped, but she was certainly in no condition for a confrontation.

And what good would it do? Thalia loved Nic, and Marcus knew. But all Dinah's proof was a fleeting expression, and what was the use of accusing Marcus of

not wanting Nic to marry her when he had never said
he did?

But she would not be taken in by the 'truce' again.
Marcus Christophi did nothing without his reasons, all
of them self-centred. If she forgot that, it would prove
she was as naïve as her father. She had looked out for
him for years, and now she would look out for herself,
saving herself from heartache.

There was a rap on the door while she was still in the
bathroom, and she answered with a towel tucked around
her. Thalia, in a short, multi-coloured jacket over a
scarlet bikini, enquired, 'Anything you need?' Orders
from Marcus, no doubt, although taking another look
at Dinah she did add, 'Are you all right?'

'Except for a headache.'

'That's the air pressure.' Thalia blew, lifting the fringe
of her own mass of hair. 'It's really over the top today.
Do you want a pain-killer?'

'Not one of Lola's,' and Thalia grinned.

'They work, but I meant a Paracetomol.'

'I've got some, thanks.'

'Take a couple. I'll get you some water.' She strolled
into the room, acting very laid-back, possibly wondering if she had told Dinah too much last night. 'We're
down by the lake,' she said. 'That OK by you? Anything
else you'd prefer to be doing?'

Thalia knew that Dinah was hardly likely to try rearranging the schedule, and Dinah said, 'Sounds lovely,'
as she found the pack of pain-killers in her purse and
shook two into her hand.

She rarely needed these but this morning she did, and
she took the glass of water from Thalia. 'You can take
some more holiday snaps,' said Thalia, looking towards
the camera on the dressing-table.

'I'm hoping to sell them,' Dinah said. 'To a photographic agency, to use in travel brochures.'

'Not to the gossip columns?'

'There's a thought.' Thalia's lips parted to speak, but instead she smiled, tight-lipped, and shook her head.

'That would be very silly,' she said very quietly. 'Now, you take it gently. Give them time to work.'

Her consideration was laid on too heavily, her dislike of Dinah was still blatant. 'Don't hurry,' she added. 'You're looking flushed—it doesn't suit you. Besides, Nic doesn't have much patience with anyone else falling sick.'

By the time Dinah had dressed in a bikini, like Thalia, with a shirt buttoned loosely over, and put on sun cream and a little make-up, the pills were slowing down the pounding. Sunbathing and swimming would suit her very well today, for it was hotter than ever. Even by the fountain, where the water rose in sparkling sprays, the atmosphere was oppressive.

The drone of the helicopter drowned the hum of the insects. She saw it hovering over, and walked to the archway at the top of the steps to watch it land. Marcus was down there on the landing pad. She took a photograph; a picture of a helicopter in these kind of surroundings might come in handy somewhere, and when three men climbed down and he shook hands with two of them she snapped again.

She recognised the third man. In Cornwall, she had overheard him talking to Marcus on the phone and met him in Nic's room. So this was probably a business meeting, and no business of hers, and she drew back, not sure whether Marcus had looked up at that moment and spotted her.

On the balcony, a breakfast buffet was laid. She was not hungry, but she sat for a while, slicing a peach and eating it slowly, drinking fruit juice and then pouring herself coffee.

When her headache had subsided into mere heaviness, she leaned over the balustrade to see Nic and Thalia sprawled below and took another picture, of the two on the rock-shelf. They were not recognisable from this angle, but it should be an attractive study, a girl and a man alone in paradise.

Thalia picked up something and handed it to Nic, rolling on to her stomach and resting her head on her folded arms. He began to rub in the oil, one-handed, and when he saw Dinah coming down the steps he gave Thalia a brisk finish and a couple of pats and called, 'Hello, darling. Do you need oiling?'

'Take your turn,' said Thalia. 'He's only done one shoulder.'

'I'm covered in cream,' said Dinah, and Nic stretched out an oily hand.

'Then come and kiss me good morning.'

She stopped to brush his mouth, and Thalia put on huge sunglasses before sitting up, so that her eyes were hidden.

'Headache better?' asked Nic.

'Do you get many headaches?' drawled Thalia. 'Perhaps you should have stayed indoors.'

'I'm perfectly fine, thank you,' said Dinah. She sat down beside Nic, who was lying full-length once more.

He said, 'It's heavy. Good excuse for being lazy.'

'Tomorrow we could go riding,' remarked Thalia. 'Into the mountains. Through the Blue Gorge.'

'Tomorrow,' said Nic.

'Or we could hitch on the helicopter and get away.'

Nic laughed then, telling Dinah, 'She misses her playmates. She soon gets bored.'

'And so do you,' Thalia pouted. 'We'll have to make up our own games, like we used to.' She turned her hidden eyes on Dinah. 'We're marooned here, you know. Usually we ship in a few friends, but this time Nic has to have peace and quiet.'

Nic yawned. 'Doctor's orders.'

'And Marc's,' said Thalia.

Dinah bit back a sharpish comment that everything seemed to come down to Marcus's orders, and said, 'Three men came in the helicopter. Aren't they friends?'

Nic and Thalia exchanged glances. 'Could be,' said Nic. 'You saw them arrive?'

'Yes. One was—Jack, is he?'

'One of the company lawyers,' said Nic.

'They don't come to play games,' said Thalia.

'The big deal?' said Dinah.

'Perhaps,' said Nic.

'Why should you care?' said Thalia, and Dinah shrugged.

'Sorry. It's none of my business.'

'You're right,' said Thalia. 'It's not.'

There was an uncomfortable silence, then Nic said placatingly, 'This is a holiday. Peace and quiet, eh?'

Dinah said, 'Of course. Anyone swimming?'

Nic was in shorts and shirt and, still incapacitated, hardly had to say, 'Not me.'

'Not yet,' said Thalia.

'Just me, then,' said Dinah, and went into the water in a shallow dive, escaping from the heat and the bickering. Almost at once she felt stronger. Her headache had gone. She had forgotten the stiffness in her neck this morning, and that seemed to have faded into nothing. She wished she could stay in the water all day, out of reach of all of them. She floated, looking up into the burning blue sky, then swam, waving when she passed the ledge of rock where Thalia, no longer in dark glasses, seemed to be following her progress.

In the heavy, still air, she heard Thalia say, 'The girl thinks she's a performing seal,' and that stopped her bobbing around on the surface. After that she went down into the depths, between the weeds that moved like strange trees in a summer breeze, glimpsing brightly coloured fish. The water was so clear that the sunlight usually reached down to the rocks and the pebbles, although dark patches showed sharply shelving fissures.

She came up several times, filling her lungs with air, then going back down again, and edging the lake were what looked like passages into the mountainside, any of which could lead into caves,

This time she was gasping when she surfaced, and Thalia was treading water nearby. 'What *are* you doing?' Thalia demanded. 'We thought you'd gone down for good.'

'No,' said Dinah, stating the obvious.

On the ledge, Nic was on his feet, shading his eyes. 'Well, come *out*,' said Thalia. 'You're making him twitchy, and it's getting on my nerves.' She set off for land in a fast crawl, and Dinah followed.

As she hauled herself out after Thalia, Nic said shrilly, 'Are you all right?'

'Yes, of course.'

'Do you know how long you were under?' He sounded as if she had gone absent without leave, although it could only have been about two minutes.

She said, 'I was all right.'

'You never told me you were a strong swimmer,' he said accusingly.

'Does it matter?' She had been swimming around for ages. It should have dawned on him by now that she was happily at home in the water.

Thalia was towelling herself and shaking her hair into a mass of wet, curling tendrils. 'You don't know much about each other, do you?' she said with open satisfaction. 'Do you have any more hidden talents?'

'Ask Marcus,' snapped Dinah. 'It should be down on my file that I can swim, but maybe it isn't down how long I can hold my breath.'

'Or your temper,' said Thalia sweetly.

After last night, Dinah had thought she was proof against Thalia's barbs, but they could still irritate. She said, in the same honeyed tones, 'I have a fairly low flashpoint, and you can put that in the file.'

'What file?' asked Nic.

'Ask Marcus,' Dinah said again. 'He had me vetted.'

That didn't seem to surprise Nic. 'Yes, I suppose he would.'

'Of course,' said Dinah. 'He thinks I'm applying for a top position in the old family firm.' Her voice came muffled from under the towel with which she was drying her hair, and when she lifted her head Nic was laughing, but she had not been joking. She found the whole idea deeply distasteful.

Nic merely said, 'I'm sure you got a clean bill.'

'So he told me, but there could still be surprises coming. For you and him.'

Nic went on smiling, and she would hate to hurt Nic. It was Marcus she wanted to stop smiling. She badly wanted to wipe the grin off his face.

They lay in the sunshine, thick towels spread beneath them. Nic's arm was across Dinah at first, but it was so hot that any touch became a burden, and she slid away. She was drowsing when she heard Thalia cry, 'Hello,' and then she rolled over and looked up to where Marcus and the man called Jack were coming down the steps.

Jack had close-cropped hair and a clever monkey face. The steel-rimmed spectacles he had worn in Cornwall were replaced by dark glasses now, and in open-necked shirt and casual trousers he looked less businesslike. Thalia jumped up, hurrying to greet him. 'Oh, I'm glad you didn't go! I thought you'd left.'

'I'm staying till morning, if you can put up with me.' That was the Boston accent that had said 'God forbid!' when Marcus had told him they could have another Carolyn situation on their hands. Of course, he knew Dinah, but he affected a vague air when Thalia said,

'This is Dinah Marsden.'

'Haven't we met before?'

Dinah said, 'Briefly. In Nic's bedroom, after the accident.'

'Of *course*.' He sounded as if he was asking himself how-could-I-have-forgotten? A sharp operator who was unlikely to forget anything, and never that he was Marcus Christophi's man. He said now, 'Nice to meet you again,' and that was another lie.

Oh, lor', thought Dinah, how cynical I'm getting!

Marcus said, 'You've been swimming?' Thalia's hair had dried into a mass of corkscrew curls that were quite fetching, but Dinah's straighter locks could well look like string.

Thalia said tartly, 'I went in to look for her. Nic thought she'd sunk without trace.'

Dinah said, 'Sorry about that. I wasn't taking any risks. I was looking for the entrance to the caves, but *only* the entrance.'

'They give me the creeps!' Thalia gave an exaggerated shudder. 'I get claustrophic even thinking about them. We haven't been down in years, have we, Nic?'

Marcus said, 'I'll take you down,' and that was un-nerving. He wanted her out of the way, and accidents can happen, she thought. Dinah knew these suspicions were fantasy, but she played for time.

'Thank you, I'd like that some time.'

'Why not now?'

As she hesitated, he watched her, eyes hooded and expressionless. Testing her? Challenging her?

'All right,' she said.

'Good.' She had made the decision he wanted, which could mean she should have said she had suddenly gone off the whole idea and wild horses would not drag her down into the lake in Marcus Christophi's wake.

Nic did raise an objection. 'I'm not sure I like you diving under the mountain. It's not always safe.'

There was her excuse, a chance to say meekly, if you don't want me to go, I won't. But she did want to see these mysterious caves. While she was here, she would be stupid to miss them.

She said, 'I've done scuba-diving and underwater photography, and I won't do anything silly. And I've had my accident quota for the month, smashing up my car on the way to the airport.'

Jack said he was sorry to hear that, and Dinah wondered if she was emphasising one recent accident so that another would be suspected. She wanted them to know she was no novice, and when the gear was brought down from the house she pushed back her hair, placed the mask against her face and inhaled. It stayed in place without support until she exhaled, when it dropped into her hands.

'That's all right,' she said, drawing the strap over the back of her head, slipping into the harness and backpack, adjusting the straps of the fins. Marcus checked her bottle clamps and webbing harness, and asked, 'Ready?'

'Sure.'

'Watch it!' Nic called as she went into the water, coming up to hold her nose and blow to clear her ears. Then she was down and away. Marcus was swimming beside her, and she was already having a wonderful time. Underwater swimming in the lake when you didn't have to keep bobbing up to breathe was magic. When Marcus signalled 'up', she followed him, exhaling, getting rid of the cylinder air in a froth of silver bubbles.

Breaking the surface, he said, 'We're going in now. The passage isn't wide and the sides are rough. It isn't far, but keep straight ahead and keep close. All right?'

She nodded happily, and he said, 'Yes, of course you're all right.' Nic was calling something. His voice reached her across the water, but she couldn't wait to listen, she had to follow Marcus. They swam down.

They went into one of the openings in the mountainside. Almost at once, the green light of the lake dimmed and darkened to indigo. Veering slightly, she brushed first one rockside then the other, and she could understand Thalia saying it was claustrophobic down here. But it was exciting too, a voyage of discovery, an adventure. And then there was shingle beneath her feet, and Marcus had her arm and she stood up.

There was air in here that must filter in somehow, and a feeling of space while she was splashing up with her webbed feet over the rocks. She could just see him as a dark shape until he turned on a torch, and then she blinked, dazzled for a moment, and pushed back her face mask.

'Some cave,' she said.

'Do you like it?'

'I'm very impressed.'

It seemed vast after the narrow tunnel, full of the sounds of water dripping and lapping. He said, 'There are lights. Sometimes they work,' and she sat on a rock, and when a light came on she clapped her hands. Other lights followed, and her gaiety changed to awe so that she sat with her hands clasped, staring around her.

When the shadows were chased away she could see more openings from the cave, each dark with its own secrets. She asked, 'Where do they all lead to?'

'They're dwellings.'

'People *lived* down here?' she croaked. 'A sort of *Atlantis*?'

'Not Atlantis.' He sounded sorry to disappoint her. 'In pre-history, when this was a settlement, there was no lake. A landslip brought flooding from the mountains that filled the valley.'

'Did they get out?' It was a question that could hardly be answered after thousands of years.

'Maybe,' he said. 'Bits of pottery are still around, but everything else has gone.' He sat down beside her, wet-skinned as she was. 'That entrance we came in by was lost until about twenty years ago. Marine archaeologists went over the caves then. No doubt they were inhabited once, there were signs of that, but for hundreds of years there have been stories of water creatures living in the lake, nereids, mermen. Come and see this.'

He stood up and she took his arm, then they clambered over the floor of the cavern towards one of the passages. This led into a much smaller cave, where torchlight shone on a fall of rock and another opening.

Marcus took off his fins and, when her fingers fumbled with the straps of hers, he stooped to unfasten them. She looked down at the big man kneeling at her feet, and had to smile again, because it was so incongruous. She said, 'They're stiff, thank you. Are we going through there?' She looked up at the rock fall, and the gap that looked about six inches wide.

'We are.'

She said mischievously, 'You'll never make it.'

'There's enough leeway.'

She pretended to plead. 'Well, *please* don't get stuck going in, or we could be in big trouble.'

'Nothing to the problem if I got stuck coming out.'

'Oh, I shall be first out!'

He laughed and held a hand to help her up the rocks. The torch sent a moving ray of light, but beyond the narrow gap it was pitch-dark. Reaching the top, he handed her the torch. He was right about getting through. He did it easily, and she leaned through to give him back the torch and then squirmed after it, landing in his arms and in another small cave.

As he turned the light, she gasped. There was a wall painting here, blue and sepia on the grey rock, a fragment of a fresco. It was of an animal, with pointed ears and a long tail, at full stretch, as if running or pouncing. 'What is it?' she whispered.

'A wildcat.'

She was entranced. It was like finding a perfect pearl in an oyster—a blue wildcat at the bottom of the lake. It must be priceless and fragile and, without touching, she traced its shape with her forefinger, entranced. She said, 'It's beautiful. Could I take a photograph?'

'I'd rather you didn't.'

'It's your cat.' It was enough to be seeing it. A blue ribbon that might have represented a river, and a pointed leaf that could have been part of a tree ended jaggedly. There was only the wildcat left.

As she stared, hardly breathing, she heard a rumbling growl and her jaw fell open. Marcus turned her towards the gap as she stammered, 'What's that?'

She was through, into the first cave, when the lights in the big cavern flickered, and he was beside her, putting her feet into her fins. The growling had followed them out, and she was confused enough to start wondering if it could be the wildcat, if they might have stirred up some ancient, atavistic force.

She could feel the rumbling all around her, like an animal stirring from sleep, and she grabbed his arm. 'What is it?'

'An earth tremor. No danger, but we'll go back now.'

He sounded casual, as though this often happened, but he held her briefly, and that was enough to quicken her chilled blood. Even when the lights went out, only leaving the torch, panic didn't paralyse her. She gasped, 'Don't worry about me. You'll have to move fast to leave me behind,' and waded alongside him, down into the tunnel entrance.

She would not let herself think that the tremor might have closed the passage. She prayed as she swam, each stroke taking her nearer the lake, and when the dark water lightened her prayers changed from 'help us' to 'thank you'.

Out of the passage and into the lake, Marcus held her arm warningly. She must not shoot up to the surface, and she nodded, going by the rules. She surfaced when he did, pushed off her mask and mouthpiece and looked up into the blue sky. 'Am I glad to be seeing that!'

The air was water-cooled, although she could feel the heat of the sun on her upturned face. 'You're a cool customer,' he said.

Not always. Now she thought about it, she wondered that she hadn't panicked. She said fervently, 'Oh, I was scared.'

'You didn't show it.'

His smile and his praise went to her head a little, making her joke, 'Screaming down there wouldn't have helped. I was waiting till I got out.'

'You're out now.'

She took in a deep breath and screamed, full throated, and the three loungers on the rock-shelf jolted upright, as if an electric shock had gone through them. As they started yelling, Marcus shouted, 'It's all right,' and Dinah waved with what she hoped were reassuring gestures.

Swimming across the lake she said, 'I suppose I shouldn't have done that.'

'It will be interesting to hear what they thought had hold of you. A giant squid or me!' Marcus grinned.

'Are there any giant squids down there?'

'None that I've come across.'

'Then I'm going to sound rather childish, screaming for fun.'

'The best of all reasons.'

She laughed. 'And very good for the lungs!' And she was still smiling when she reached the ledge and was unceremoniously hauled up by the three of them.

'What happened?' Nic's anxious face was thrust into hers as she struggled to sit upright, encumbered by gear.

'Nothing.'

'Then what were you screaming at?' Thalia snapped.

Marcus, getting out of his own harness and backpack, said 'There was an earth tremor while we were down there. That was the scream she didn't have time for in the caves.'

As soon as they knew that the bloodcurdling shriek was Dinah fooling around, Thalia and Nic lost patience. Nic howled, 'That was a bloody stupid thing to do!'

And Thalia rolled exasperated eyes, muttering, 'Every time you go swimming, you give us heart attacks.'

'No need,' said Marcus. 'Dinah can look after herself.'

That was what she had told herself last night. That was what she must remember, to look out for herself.

The harness fell from her and she picked up the nearest towel, feeling again the suffocating heaviness of the air.

Nic was looking as disapproving as Thalia. The likeness between them was marked.

Jack glanced first at Marc, then at Dinah, and Dinah said, 'I'm going to shower.' Suddenly, she needed to be alone. She slipped into her shirt and sandals, picked up her camera and said, 'Back soon.'

She was in the courtyard when she heard the footsteps, and when she turned it was Jack. He was heading for the office, but she crossed over to him and asked, 'Why are you sorry for me?'

'You're mistaken!' He guffawed with embarrassed laughter.

'I don't think so. That was a poor-cow look you gave me just now, so what is so pathetic about me?'

He hesitated, and she reminded herself that he was a Christophi man, so what could she learn from him? But then he said, 'You seem a nice girl and you're getting a raw deal. Marcus is never going to let Nic marry you. You're wasting your time here.'

'Did he tell you that?' She meant about Marcus, and Jack shrugged, then she drawled, 'Oh, I reckon I'll hang around.'

He took off his sunglasses and his eyes were like steel, but he sounded as if he was still sorry for her when he said, 'Your description, lady, but you *are* a poor little cow who hasn't a clue what she's up against.'

CHAPTER SEVEN

As JACK strode off towards the office, Dinah went into her bedroom. His outburst was no news to her. She knew that Marcus did not intend her to marry Nic, but when she was alone with Marcus it was hard to remember he was an antagonist. What she was up against was the risk of relaxing her guard. She had not needed Jack to tell her she could not win.

She could leave in the morning, but that would be quitting too soon, and there were always photographs to be taken. She could start looking on her stay as a professional assignment, keeping an eye open for good shots and a firm hold on her emotions. It would not be the first time she had relegated her worries to the back of her mind, but that was easier in a cooler climate. Here, the atmosphere made her feel like a small, seething volcano, needing very little more stress to blow its top.

She showered, washed her hair and lay on her bed in a skimpy cotton slip. Languidly, she recorded details about the photographs she had taken today, making them short and impersonal, in case the tapes fell into other hands. She did not want anyone hearing what she thought about anyone here, although they were quick enough passing opinions on her.

It was no compliment being told you were a poor cow, even if you had said it first. And coming from a man who looked like a monkey, it was a cheek. That photograph of Jack getting out of the helicopter this morning—she hoped it didn't flatter him. If he looked ugly enough, she might send him a copy, but right now she didn't care if she never saw any of them again.

There was no reason to rush back to join them. It was nicer here than stretching out on the rocks under a barrage of critical eyes. Nic might come looking for her eventually, but nobody else would, and she was feeling sorry for herself, although self-pity had never been her style. What am I doing here? she thought. Why am I letting this happen?

It could be the heat, settling on her like a black cloud. If it got too bad, she could always get out. No one would keep her here if she wanted to leave. Marcus would let her go. But not yet. She would sweat it out for a few more days, if only to show Marcus what she was made of.

All that swimming had tired her, and now she tried to recapture the sensation of gliding through deep, cool water, until at last she slipped into a dreaming sleep.

She called, 'Come in,' drowsily when she heard the tap on the door. She was hardly awake yet. Her eyes were half closed, so that she saw Marcus in the doorway through her long, dark lashes. That made her sit up and grab for a sheet, glaring at him over the top of it.

'Are you all right?' he enquired.

'I fell asleep.'

He turned away. 'They're coming in now.'

'What am I supposed to do about it?'

'You could put some clothes on.' He sounded as if he was smiling, obviously thinking that Nic might have strolled into her room.

She called after him, 'Thanks for warning me, I don't want to raise anyone's temperature. There must be a real risk of going up in flames in this heat.'

She heard him laugh as she jumped out of bed and shut the door. A few minutes later it was Nic tapping.

By then she was dressed and dragging a comb through her hair. 'Why are you hiding yourself in here?' he asked.

'I've been asleep.' Her washed hair had dried tangled, she realised.

Nic said, 'If I'd known I'd have come and woken you.'

'Too late,' she replied; Marcus had seen to that.

'I fell asleep myself. We could have snuggled up together.'

She put down the comb and tried her luck with a brush. The tangles hurt. Vigorous brushing was making her hotter than ever, and she said tetchily, 'The only man I could snuggle up to right now would be a snowman.'

'Thalia said you were sulking because I swore at you.'

'Thalia is talking nonsense as usual.'

'Well,' said Nic maddeningly, 'something isn't agreeing with you, and what have you done to your hair?'

She couldn't deny it looked a mess. She said sweetly, 'I'll join you in ten minutes. By then I'll have brushed my hair, and I'll try to be a credit to you.'

Nobody here thought she could ever be good enough for Nic, but she was stupid to let that make her so irritable, and she would behave herself for what was left of today.

Not long afterwards, with her hair smoothed, and looking as amiable as she could manage, she followed the voices. She came upon them all in a big room, air-conditioned to a tolerable temperature although, even in here, there was a strange heaviness in the air.

The walls were marble and the furniture was beautiful, of course. It must have been a problem getting this lot up all those precipitous bends. Or would the bigger pieces, like the grand piano, be airlifted in? Dinah wondered.

Marcus was standing by a window, a little way away. Jack and Nic and Thalia were grouped together, and Nic patted a stool beside him. Nobody else looked at Dinah as she trotted over and tucked herself on to it, placing her camera at her feet.

Thalia just went on with some tale she was telling, mimicking somebody's high, nasal voice, keeping Nic and Jack chuckling. Dinah smiled politely, the outsider. As she didn't know who they were talking about, Thalia's act didn't have much point for her. Then the three of them were laughing together, and Jack said, wiping his eyes, 'I don't want to be around if he ever hears you do that take-off.'

Marc had his back to them, but when Thalia asked suddenly, 'Do you sleep with that thing, Dinah?' he turned.

She was pointing to the camera case, and Dinah admitted, 'Nearly. I like it by me. I feel lost without it.'

Thalia's eyes gleamed wickedly. 'What sort of goings-on do you snap in the night? Watch it, Nic, that holiday album could be riotous!' And Dinah blushed, acutely uncomfortable.

Marc said, 'Jack can take any films you've finished back in the morning and get them developed for you,' and she had to explain that she preferred to handle her work from start to finish.

'What *have* you got on film, if you daren't let it go?' cried Thalia. 'Have you got a market lined up?'

'Of course,' said Dinah. 'A girl has to live.'

It got no easier. They sat down to a meal that filled the table: tiny cheese and spinach pasties, great dishes of seafood—squid, octopus, prawns—raw artichokes, miniature meatballs, dips and salads. Dinah ate without appetite, and drank cold wine and fruit juice because her throat was parched.

'What would you like to do tomorrow?' Nic asked her, refilling her glass.

'Anything,' she replied.

'Keep out of the caves,' said Marcus, 'until we're sure that tremor was an isolated incident.'

'And not, as Lola would say, because the old ones are stirring.' Nic dropped his voice to a melodramatic throb and grinned, and they all smiled, because they knew old Lola, with her spells and her sayings. Even Jack, who was a confidential friend, as well as one of the firm, sure enough of himself to warn Dinah that she did not belong here. As if that was not being made clearer to her all the time!

'We could go riding,' said Thalia. 'You do ride, I suppose?'

'If you mean a horse, not a bike,' said Dinah, 'not really. I've jogged around in a meadow, and that was about it.'

'Oh, dear, we'll have to find you a nice old nag,' said Thalia, and Dinah could visualise that scene. Of course Thalia and Nic would be superb on horseback, while she would be bouncing about like a sack of potatoes, falling off probably, and looking a complete idiot.

She took another gulp of wine, met Marcus's eyes and said, 'Sorry to disappoint you, but no thanks.'

'Very wise,' he said.

'You could always stay at the farmhouse,' said Thalia, presumably while she and Nic rode off, but if Nic didn't object Dinah was darned if she would. 'So, who *is* coming riding?' asked Thalia and Marcus shook his head. 'Jack? Can't you stay?'

She put her pretty face close to his, her soft red lips pouted invitingly, but he said, 'I can't. I wish I could.'

'Isn't business a *bore*?' The pout changed from provocative to petulant.

'Not when Marcus is around,' said Jack. And soon after that the two men stood up, leaving the table still covered with food, and Dinah wishing she could follow them.

Not to go with them, of course, but to get out of this room and away from Thalia, who was surely going to cause trouble.

There had been no flare-up while Marcus was in the room, but she seemed as jumpy as Dinah felt. As soon as the door closed behind them, she said, 'What do we do now? Three's such an awkward number.' She drained her glass and chanted, 'Two's company. Three's none. Four's all right, if two walk on.'

It was years since Dinah had heard that childish jingle, and Nic said mildly, 'Steady with the ouzo.'

'We could have a sing-song,' said Thalia, sounding more than slightly inebriated. 'Do you sing? Do you play?'

'Neither,' said Dinah.

'But you do take a lot of photographs. How did those you took in Cornwall turn out?'

'Quite well, thank you.'

'Can we see them?' Nic asked.

'They got glued together with something tacky when my case was squashed.'

'What a shame,' said Thalia with exaggerated mournfulness. 'So we've only your word for it that they were any good at all.'

There was no answer to that. Dinah flung out her hands, palms upwards, with a take-it-or-leave it grimace, and Thalia stared hard at her, as if she was still trying to work out what Nic found so attractive. Then she asked, 'Do you always tell the truth?'

'I try,' said Dinah and thought, I've had enough of this. She shifted in her seat to stand up, but Thalia was on her feet first, beckoning.

'Come and look,' she demanded walking towards a mirror on the far wall. It had a wide, gilt baroque frame, ornate and old, and Thalia pulled out a chair and set it squarely in front of the mirror, saying 'Do sit down.'

'Why not?' Dinah sat, facing her own angry eyes and set jawline, with the long, elegant room as background. Nic was still lounging in his chair at the table, watching them, and Thalia talked to Dinah in the mirror.

'This is the truth mirror,' she said solemnly. 'Lola's glass. When we were children, she told us that if we lied while we were looking in here the glass would darken.'

'No home should be without one,' Dinah muttered.

'It can happen,' whispered Thalia.

Of course it had, when they were children, with old Lola standing behind them. To an imaginative child with a guilty conscience, the shadows would seem to fall thick and fast.

'So tell us,' said Thalia, 'did Nic really ask you to marry him?'

Nic got up and Dinah said, 'Yes.'

'Do you really love him?' Thalia moved closer to the mirror, peering into it. The girl couldn't actually be expecting a reaction in there, could she?

'Yes,' said Dinah.

'More than you could ever love any other man?'

She meant Marcus. She knew how he was trying to get Dinah away from Nic, and she thought Dinah might hesitate now. Any indecision would hurt Nic's pride.

And Dinah *had* hesitated, because that was the final dig that blew her control.

She turned in the chair, grabbing Thalia's arm hard, 'It won't work for me,' she said through gritted teeth, 'because I know it's a load of rubbish. If you're the believer, you're the one to play the truth game. You look in the glass and tell us—do you love Nic more than you could ever love any other man? Is that why you can't stand the sight of me, because you want Nic? And not as a brother, because he isn't your brother.'

The chair had gone flying. Dinah was on her feet with a grip on Thalia that forced her to face the mirror, and Thalia was writhing and screeching, 'Let go of me!'

'Isn't that the truth?'

Thalia began to laugh so that her hair fell over her face, and she threw back her head, still laughing, spluttering, 'That is the funniest thing I have ever heard.'

'I've heard funnier,' said Dinah.

Hot anger was bubbling in her, and Nic was there with a rough hand on her shoulder, shouting, 'What the hell are you playing at?'

'Some game.' Thalia finally wriggled free. 'One thing's for sure, Dinah, you can't take a joke.'

Thalia had sobered up. Her voice was no longer even slightly slurred, and her eyes were clear and overbright as she rubbed her arm where Dinah had grabbed her and gasped, 'The girl's a savage.'

'I'm sorry.' Dinah knew that she was not sounding sorry, but that scuffle had been a mistake. She could have said what she wanted to say without a wrestling match, and what she *had* said had been wasted breath. Nic didn't believe it, and Dinah could have been wrong. Maybe Thalia did think of Nic as a brother, and simply did not want Dinah as a sister.

'Do you often have brainstorms?' Thalia made a big show of pushing her hair into place and smoothing her dress down, drawling, 'I'll leave you two alone. We mustn't upset Dinah. If she's jealous of me, it shows a very suspicious nature.' She twisted her upper arm for another look. 'I'm getting a bruise there. Don't play any more parlour games with her, Nic, she could do you an injury. Wait till you get your right arm working.'

'And what was that exhibition about?' Nic demanded coldly, as soon as they were alone. His nostrils were flared, his lips had a scornful curl, and Dinah thought that he looked as if he was getting a whiff from some very unpleasant drains.

She said, 'I guess I can't take a joke. Or I can't stand the climate. I don't know about brainstorms, but I could do with a rainstorm. And now I'd like to go to my room, so please would you excuse me?'

It was a bit late for good manners, but she walked fast down the long salon, scooping up her camera and hoping Nic would say nothing to stop her, because she felt that she had eaten too much and drunk too much and said too much.

He let her go without a word, and she reached her room without meeting anyone else. All the doors into the courtyard were closed, shutting her out if she had had any mad idea of following Marcus into the office. She hadn't a friend in the place. Even Nic was seeing her in a disturbing light that surprised her as much as it did him. She didn't like this Dinah, either.

She had said too much just now, but what she had drunk had been mainly fruit juice. Nor had she eaten too much, because now she felt hollow and aching with loneliness, and writing to Barbara did not dispel her isolation.

She sat at a little bureau, using the stationery in a drawer, and rambled on, starting with her car crash and a reassurance that she had come out of that without a scratch. She gave Barbara the name of the garage, and said that Marcus Christophi had said he would deal with it, but please would Barbara ring through and check that he had remembered?

She told Barbara about Lola's potions and how magnificent the villa was. She wrote, 'All I'm doing is lying in the sun and swimming in the lake and taking photographs. There is talk of horse riding tomorrow, but not for me. Too risky and too steep round here.' She managed to fill three pages, and put down her pen at the end of it feeling like a castaway with a letter she hoped to despatch in a bottle.

But if Jack would post this on the mainland in the morning it should reach Barbara before too long. And, next morning, it was the sound of the helicopter that roused her. She had slept badly of course, and today she was determined to cause no more scenes. She would stay calm if it killed her. She would not think beyond today, and she would take today as it came.

Across the courtyard, the office door was open, so that the first person she saw was Marcus. He came towards her where she stood near the fountain, and she was glad he hadn't witnessed last night's little tussle, or he would have realised that the fresco in the lake was not the only wildcat around.

'Good morning,' he said.

'Have you been there all night?' she asked.

'Not quite.'

'Would Jack post this for me?' She held out her letter and he took it. She was breathing shallowly. Being close to him often made her breathless, as if she was waiting for something.

When Nic touched her, she jumped. She hadn't heard him coming, and that was something else Marcus did. Her awareness got centred on him, so that everyone else seemed to walk and talk softly.

But Nic's voice was loud and cheery. 'Morning, darling!' And his smile was forgiving. 'Are you all right?'

She said she was. She said, 'About last night——'

'Forget it,' said Nic. 'It's the heat. Doesn't seem to suit you up here.' She thought he looked jaded himself, in spite of his grin. He told her, 'I'm going with Jack. I've some business to see to in Crete. I'll bring the *Condor* back to Styros, and meet you there tomorrow and we'll cruise around the islands.'

'How do I get to the harbour?'

'Marc's bringing you and Thalia. It's all arranged.'

Marcus had gone through the archway. She watched his tall figure walking away from her, out of the villa, and she said, 'Yes it sounds lovely.'

She would go along quietly with any arrangements, she had no energy this morning, and an ocean-going cruise *did* sound like a marvellous idea.

'I'll have a surprise for you tomorrow,' Nic said, and when she looked at him enquiringly he tipped her chin and kissed her lips, then said, 'Trust me. I've got to go now.'

If she hadn't walked out, he wouldn't even have said goodbye. Marc would have told her about the arrangements, and she wondered if Nic was dashing off on Marc's instructions. She sat down on the white marble ridge of the fountain, dabbling her hand in water that was warm as her skin.

The sky above was clear as ever, except for one cloud hanging low over the mountain range. After a while she saw the helicopter rise and hover, and watched the black dot vanish into blue space before she turned her head to look at Marcus, who was standing beside her.

His expression was quizzical, so perhaps he *had* heard about her 'brainstorm'. 'Well?' she said.

'I was wondering why you didn't want to go with him.'

There hadn't been time. She hadn't had a chance to think about it. But she had had no instinctive pang because Nic was off somewhere without her. 'He didn't ask me,' she said.

She hadn't wanted to go, anyway. She looked back at the cloud, the colour of dark smoke and quite still. Thalia came out of her room and called, 'Has Jack gone?'

'Nic went with him,' said Marcus, and that brought her hurrying sandal heels clacking on the mosaic floor. 'He's calling at Heraklion, and we're joining him on the *Condor*.'

Thalia wailed, 'Why did nobody wake me? I'd have gone, too. Has he gone to the works?'

'Yes,' said Marcus, and Thalia went on frowning until Marcus was back in the office.

'And how's your health and temper this morning?' she asked Dinah.

A bit like that cloud, Dinah could have said—dark and heavy, and out of place. She said softly, to herself rather than to Thalia, 'What is it doing up there in a clear sky?' and then Thalia looked towards the mountaintop.

'I wouldn't know,' she said. 'Why don't you take a photograph of it? It doesn't seem to be going anywhere.'

The day wore on in a strange hush. If Dinah was leaving tomorrow, this was her last chance for taking photographs. She strolled around, getting a few shots that might make the travel brochures, but all the time feeling so wrung-out that everything was too much trouble. Food was served on the balcony, and Dinah ate little and alone. She saw Lola and Ireni and several men going about their chores, quiet as shadows. She didn't see Marcus at all, and Thalia seemed to spend the day lolling around in the big salon.

Dinah kept out of there after she wandered in and was met by Thalia's glare. They had nothing to say to each other, and it was evening before she exchanged another word with anyone.

She was yawning as she showered and changed, although she had dozed during the afternoon. She would need to borrow a case or a bag to pack her few belongings in the morning, and tonight she put on the yellow dress again.

When she came out into the open air of the courtyard, the cloud had not moved. Nor had it changed shape. She gasped, 'I don't believe it, you're still there!'

'Believe it,' murmured Marcus.

He was standing, shaded by the wistaria tree, smoking a thin cigar, and a smile curved her lips at the sight of him. 'Not you,' she said. 'That cloud up there. It hasn't moved all day, didn't you see it?'

'I've been in the office all day. Clearing up business before we go off in the *Condor*.'

'You're coming?' It shouldn't matter to her, but all the same she was pleased to hear it.

'You're not getting rid of me that easily.' His smile glinted and she wrinkled her nose.

'How many of those things do you smoke?'

'Why?'

Why, indeed? It was none of her business, and she shook her head. 'Just making small talk. It's been a funny day; you're the first one I've spoken to since morning. You lose the knack. You start asking nosy questions.'

Suddenly she was feeling cheerful, glad to have someone to joke with.

'Do you mind it?' he asked.

'Not a bit, it's almost agreeable,' she declared chirpily.

'Good,' he said, 'because this is the least of my vices.'

It was good to laugh, walking beside him towards the salon, hearing a piano being played. 'Is that Thalia?' she asked.

'Yes.'

'She plays beautifully.' Like a concert pianist. 'What is it?' Dinah was not up on classical music, she didn't recognise this piece, with its complicated swoops and trills.

'A Chopin concerto. One of Nic's favourites.' If he had expected her to know that, it showed again how little she *did* know of Nic. As she entered the room, Thalia brought her performance to an end, hands down in a crashing discord. She was not playing for Dinah, and compliments on her skill would not be graciously received, so Dinah said nothing.

Thalia took a seat at the table, Marc poured an aperitif into fluted glasses and they began their meal. Stuffed aubergines for starters, followed by sea bass, colourful with parsley, tomato and green peppers. Dinah thought, I must remember these dishes, so that I can try them out at home when my holiday is over.

In contrast to last night, Thalia hardly spoke during dinner. Talk was mostly about the route they would take on board the *Condor*. Marc described the islands. He told her their histories, answered her questions, and she listened, enthralled, already there in her imagination.

When the lights flickered, she needed a moment to adjust. As she blinked, they steadied again, and Thalia said, 'Hell!'

It had to be a generator up here, there wouldn't be electricity cables. Marc said, 'We could be in for a storm.'

'Not for me, thank you very much,' said Thalia tartly. 'I'll take an early night and a nightcap.' She picked up a decanter.

Marc said 'Goodnight' quietly and Thalia gave him a wry smile.

'See you in the morning,' she said.

There was a Georgian candelabra on the piano, and Marc brought it and a lighter to the table. So there *was* a danger that the lights might go out, thought Dinah. But they went on with their meal, discussing photographs Dinah might get on the islands.

'What have you taken today?' he enquired.

'Just the scenes around the villa. Nothing thrilling. One of Lola when she wasn't looking.' She had an almond cream decorated with strawberries before her, and she bit into a small, sweet berry. 'I didn't ask her in case she put the evil eye on my camera.'

'You think she could do that?' He was fooling and so was she, turning towards the big mirror on the far wall.

'You tell me, does the truth mirror work?' He looked blank and she went on, 'Did it go dark when you were young?' Her eyes danced. 'Forgive me, I mean younger. Or did Thalia make it up?'

Then he remembered and chuckled. 'I was past believing in magic when Lola came up with that idea, but it seemed to work on them. What did they tell you?'

She would only have told him enough to keep him smiling, but as she began, 'Well——' she heard a sound in the silence, like the growling of an animal. She gasped, 'What's that?'

'Thunder.' Of course it was thunder, followed almost immediately by a flash of lightning, and within seconds by another, bathing the room in brilliant white light.

Then there was blackness and the lighter flared, and Marcus touched the four long-stemmed candles. As the flames took hold, burning steadily, there was shouting. 'Come on,' he said, although Dinah was hardly likely to stay here eating her almond cream.

She said, as she had in the caves, 'You'll have to move fast to leave me behind.'

'I wouldn't do that,' he said, or she thought that was what he said, because there was a babble of raised voices. When they neared the courtyard, torches were flashing.

Marcus blew out the candles, left the candelabra in the passageway, and went over to the office with one of the men who was carrying a torch. Standing in the doorway, Dinah heard the crackle of static from the radio receiver—no contact was being made there. She whirled round as lightning exploded overhead, lasting long enough to show them still as statues: Lola and Ireni, the men, and Thalia in the open doorway of her bedroom.

Marcus came out of the office and they all turned towards him, and then it was pitch-dark again, except for the torches. Lola wailed something high and shrill, and Marc said a few words that sounded both an order and a reassurance, and then they were trooping away.

Thalia was beside Dinah, who gasped, 'Where are we going?'

'Into the cellars.'

'What did Lola say?'

'Something is coming.'

'Not up from the lake, I hope,' Dinah muttered, and she felt Thalia's convulsive grip on her arm. The two girls stumbled along together.

The heavy, studded door to the cellars opened on to a steep flight of steps cut in rock, leading into caves. Marcus stood at the top, shepherding them down, closing the door and following them. Down below, torchlight illuminated dusty wine-racks, reaching from floor to roof, running into the shadows of the interior; and the little group gathered away from the racks in a small, buttressed recess.

The language was Greek, and there was no interpreting. Dinah stood with her back pressed against the rock and her fingers laced tightly together, and was thankful that nobody seemed to be panicking. However, she would have felt happier if Lola and Ireni had not kept crossing themselves. Marcus was calm enough to look relaxed, but that meant nothing, and Dinah turned to Thalia, who was pale in the dim light.

'Do you come down here often?' she got out shakily.

'Only when the old ones are stirring,' said Thalia, and her laugh was wobbly.

'Just my luck,' said Dinah. 'I never go anywhere without my camera, but I haven't got it now, so I could miss the shot of a lifetime,' and they laughed a little, both scared, huddling together.

A man shouted, and instinctively everybody moved closer to their own. Marc's arms were around Dinah and Thalia, his body shielding them. Then a roaring like a jet-plane made Dinah cover her ears and press her face hard against his chest.

She didn't know whether the cellars were shaking, or whether the shaking was inside her, nor how long Marc held her, until voices could be heard again and he said, 'It's passed us.'

They were all chattering now, laughing and hugging each other. Thalia whispered, 'Will it come back?'

'It must be nearly played out this far inland,' replied Marc.

If that was on the wane, Dinah thought, what was it like in full flush? She croaked, 'What was it?'

'A whirlwind,' said Marcus. 'A tornado. Wait here.'

He took a torch and went up the steps. As the door at the top opened, Dinah ran after him, although the rest stood waiting. Now everything was still again, still and silent, and the torchlight showed no cracks in the walls, no structural damage.

They came up when Marcus called them, and as the last man appeared at the top of the stairs the rains started. Thalia ran towards the courtyard, Lola and Ireni and their menfolk the other way. Marcus took Dinah's arm and followed Thalia, and in the open courtyard the downpour was already heavy enough to drench them before they reached the shelter of Thalia's room.

With the door closed, there was no light from the window, just a dark torrent of water, pouring down, and now Dinah understood the urgency to get out of the cellars. It was no comfort to remember that the villa was built on the mountainside.

Any minute now, she thought, I could start screaming, and she heard Thalia first whimper and then burst into tears.

Marcus held her, hushing her like a child, and she sobbed against him. 'Nic's on the *Condor*. He's at sea. Oh, God, Marc, is Nic all right?'

'He'll be all right,' said Marcus, and Thalia twisted her head to look around at Dinah, her voice unnaturally calm, on the edge of hysteria.

'They come up from the sea, you know. This one must have started off the coastline, and the *Condor*'s a little boat. Well, not as motor-cruisers go, but it would have to be a bloody great liner to stand much chance. Can't we get through to somebody and find out where Nic is?'

Marcus said gently, 'No.' He released her, and she sat on the edge of her bed, rocking to and fro like a child. He had laid the torch down on the dressing-table when he came into the room, and by its light he poured from the decanter into the glass beside it. 'Drink this.'

'This won't stop for hours, will it?' She went on rocking.

'Probably not.'

'I could be out of my mind by then.' She reached for the glass, anxious for oblivion, gulping, coughing, gulping again and handing it back empty. Then she lay down and turned her face away.

Marc touched the decanter and looked at Dinah, but she shook her head. If the storm did undermine the villa, staying sober wouldn't help, they would all go over the cliffs and down the mountainside, but she wanted to stay aware. When he smiled at her, she managed to smile back.

They would not be able to leave this room for hours. She couldn't stay soaking wet and chilled as she had never expected to be on the island. She said, 'I'm taking this dress off, do you mind? Can I borrow something?'

There was no reply from Thalia, so Dinah slipped off her dress and put on another from the rail. Marcus was still in the shirt that clung wetly to him, sitting on a sofa placed for enjoying the view from the windows. But there was no view tonight.

Dinah sat beside him and said, 'Shouldn't you get out of that?' She smiled again as she said it, because a damp shirt was not going to bother him.

He said, 'I don't want to walk out of here half naked, it might look as if I slipped the chaperon a Mickey Finn.' And Dinah found herself laughing for real.

However, there was little to laugh at yet. As well as the torrential rain, great hailstones were crashing against the windows, and she asked softly, so as not to disturb Thalia, 'Does this kind of thing happen often?'

His voice was quiet, too. 'Styros was a volcanic island once. Storms are common enough, but a tornado is a rare bird. Altogether, this has been a memorable summer.'

She said, '*I* shall remember it.' She looked into his face, the hooded eyes and the strong, sensual mouth, and knew that she would remember him as long as she lived. And she heard herself say quite gaily, 'Is Lola any good at stopping storms?'

'Going by this, I shouldn't think so.'

'Not a witch for the weather? I suppose it could be me. I wished for rain last night.'

'Then you don't know your own strength.' She had never seen rain like it, the wonder was that the windows were holding. The glass might be toughened, but the hailstones looked as big as tennis balls. 'Witchcraft is one thing,' said Marcus solemnly, 'but this is excessive.'

'Going over the top is the least of my vices,' sighed Dinah.

He laughed and told her, 'It's as well we don't have a room for two!'

Although she knew they were in peril and she would be stupid not to be scared, she was suddenly sure she was coming through. When she asked him, 'You believe we are going to be all right?' she knew he would say yes, and that she would believe him.

The foundations of the villa were rock. Having withstood the winds, it would also withstand the rain pouring down the mountainside into the lake and out beyond. From the courtyard there would be a waterfall down the flight of steps, swirling in and carrying on through any opened doors, but the doors that were closed would be holding. There seemed no build-up on this one.

She listened, saying nothing of things they could do nothing about until they got out of here. Such as, was everyone else in the villa safe? What destruction had the tornado left in its wake, and where was the *Condor*? And no mention of the rain against the windows, making

it look as if they were already beneath the lake. She
wondered if the water creatures were waiting for them.

Marc held her hands as he talked, and she appeared
very calm. 'I don't think staring at the window is going
to help,' he said finally.

'I was getting bored with the programme, let's change
channels,' she replied.

He lifted the sofa round to face the room, placed a
couple of cushions at one end and said, 'Put your feet
up and close your eyes.'

'*Sleep?* I couldn't. Look at it, listen to it!'

He pulled blinds down, dropped another cushion on
an oriental rug beside the sofa and stretched out, arms
under his head. 'I'll wake you when it's over,' he said.
'There'll be work to do.'

She sat, feet up on the sofa, and looked down at him.
The house felt safe and solid, and she hoped the torch
battery would last. She thought, I could have night-
mares, and remembered that nightmare in Cornwall when
he had been stalking her and she had been frantic to
escape from him. 'If I fall asleep,' she said, 'don't you
go anywhere without me.'

For some of that night she slept. The rain fell, re-
lentless and unceasing. She heard it every time she
listened, and more than once Thalia woke sobbing, only
to sleep again when Marcus spoke softly to her. When
he came back to Dinah, she said, 'I'm fine.' And in a
crazy way she was, as though having him beside her in
the darkness of the room meant that all would be well
in the morning. She could have touched him by stretching
out a hand, and because of that she could sleep.

Then she woke, with a grey light in her eyes. The blinds
were up and the rain was stopping. She was beside Marc
as he opened the door into the courtyard. The skies
overhead were leaden, the mosaic floor awash, the

fountain bowl running over. The great wistaria had been stripped, its boughs were dripping and bare, and one of the statues had crashed from its plinth.

'Not so bad,' said Marcus.

'When did it stop?'

'A few minutes ago.'

A bleak dawn was breaking, and it *wasn't* so bad, because they all came hurrying from wherever they had sheltered. Dinah, feeling punch-drunk, wandered around looking for her camera, mildly surprised to find it in her bedroom and undamaged. She should be out after news pictures. She should be out offering to mop up or prop up or whatever needed to be done, and she put on a white cotton jacket, because it was almost cool this morning.

She heard the helicopter and clasped her hands, praying it would bring news that Nic was safe. It must have been near, circling the storm area, desperate to land here. She went to her bedroom door as Marcus came into the courtyard, and heard Nic shouting, 'Marc! Thalia!'

Thank God, she thought. She saw the two men meet, Nic stumbling against Marc.

'The road's down. There's a hell of a lot of damage. I thought you might have gone riding or driving or——' He stopped; something had stopped him. He was looking into Marc's face and his voice was strangled. 'Where's Thalia?'

Marc said nothing, and Nic threw back his head and screamed her name. Her door opened and Thalia flew out. No one looked Dinah's way. Nic and Thalia had eyes only for each other; their arms were around each other, Thalia sobbing, Nic gabbling her name over and over. 'Thalia! Oh, Thalia! Oh, my love...oh, Thalia...'

Marc stood suddenly even taller, as if a weight had fallen from his shoulders. Then he turned towards Dinah, and she said, 'Don't say you're sorry for me. Don't say anything.'

'*Dinah!*' Nic had literally forgotten her until she spoke. She was nothing here. It was finished.

'It's all right,' she said. She was still facing Marcus, and her heart felt like a lump of lead. 'Can I go home now?'

CHAPTER EIGHT

DINAH stepped back into her room, closing the door behind her. She crossed to the window and stared into a world that seemed washed out into varying shades of grey.

When the door opened and closed again, she knew without turning that it was Marcus. She said 'I never had a chance with Nic. You never meant us to have a chance. What a charade it's been!' She sounded shrill as she spun round to face him. 'All this trouble, and I *have* been a lot of trouble to you. If this hadn't shown him how he feels about Thalia, would you have told him we slept together last night?'

'Quite possibly,' he said, and that took her breath away, although now everything was settled the way he wanted there was no need to make himself agreeable any longer. From now on, she could hate his guts and it wouldn't worry him. And she did.

'Well, congratulations, and I hope they'll be very happy,' she said. She thought they would, but she couldn't find words for what she hoped for him. 'And when I get home I shall write in big letters on my bedroom wall, where I can see it first thing in the morning and last thing at night, "Never trust big, bossy men." I should have remembered that from the beginning.'

He said harshly, 'Don't be childish.' But knowing how silly she was sounding only made her more belligerent, and she might even have started throwing things if Nic had not walked in.

He looked dreadful, haggard with guilt. His 'Please can I speak to you?' sounded as if he expected a torrent of abuse. But she was not angry with Nic. He had made a mistake, but there had been no cold-blooded conniving.

She said, 'Of course,' and to Marcus, picking up the pocket recorder, 'Would you like this turned on so that you can have a record? You wouldn't want anything going on you didn't know about.'

He made no reply, for she was being childish again. As he closed the door behind him, Nic said miserably, 'I don't know what to say.'

'You said it out there.' She nearly put her arms around him, he looked so worried. It would only have been a sisterly hug, but better not, she decided, so she put the warmth into her voice, assuring him, 'It's all right. I think you're right for each other.'

He was so grateful for her understanding that the confidences spilled out. 'You *did* know. That business with the mirror. Until you said that, I never realised how our feelings for each other had changed since we were kids. It kept me awake all night, and by morning I thought, no, Thalia isn't in love with you. Thalia thought it was a joke, she laughed about it. It's Dinah, I thought, of course it is. I went to the workshop and picked out a ring for you. I was going to give it to you on the *Condor*. But when I heard about the weather conditions out here, boats were staying in harbour, and we came in the chopper first chance... and I knew it was Thalia.' The memory of the ordeal of waiting silenced him, then he said huskily, 'I'm sorry, but it was.'

And Marcus had prolonged the agony long enough for him to believe he had lost Thalia. Dinah said, 'I hope the ring fits.'

He dug a hand into his pocket, coming out with a ring box, offering eagerly, 'Would you have it?'

'No, thank you.' She wanted no keepsake from this affair. Her gesture stopped him even opening the box, and when she asked, 'What has happened out there?' he put it back in his pocket.

Offering her what should have been an engagement ring had been tactless. There was nothing mercenary about Dinah. He said, 'It wasn't one of the biggest. They can cut a path over a mile wide, this one is less. It's driven boats inland and smashed through the groves. Seems to have missed the villages, but buildings have gone and the road's sheered away.'

He looked towards the door, anxious to tell Thalia how decent Dinah was being. Also, there had to be something he could do in the aftermath of the whirlwind, even if he was hardly fighting fit yet.

'I'd like to be alone for a while,' said Dinah. She did not want Thalia arriving next. Nic said he understood and bless her, and they would see her later.

There was no water from taps, cisterns were not working, but the fountain bowl was full of rainwater. Dinah slipped out and scooped up a jugful, then washed in it. The helicopter took off and returned within the half-hour, and she went out then, because she had to face them, and walked straight into Thalia, who was sweeping out the courtyard, and waiting for Dinah to emerge going by the speed with which she dropped the broom and rushed over, asking, 'Are you all right?'

'Of course.'

'I can't say I'm sorry, you'd know it wasn't true, but I wish it hadn't taken a tornado. We were all shaken to pieces. Except for Marc, and nothing ever shakes him!' She gave a nervous smile, and gabbled, 'But it was pretty awful how it happened, and I'm sorry about that. I only wish there was something I could do.'

To make amends for Nic forgetting Dinah's existence? Thalia had enough sympathy for the other girl to wish that the break had been less brutal, and Dinah said, 'That tornado got his priorities right for him, so don't knock it. And there is something you can do for me. Get me out of here.'

'Don't you want to take photographs?'

'Not half as much as I want to go home.' It was probably the first time her job was not taking priority.

Thalia bit her lip. 'Marc gave orders you were to stay here.' Marcus and Nic had gone to the farm where the horses were stabled. From there, they might move anywhere along the whirlwind's trail. Thalia had been told to stay where she was, for there was plenty to be done around the villa, and Dinah was to be discouraged from roaming alone with her camera. On no account was she to leave the vicinity. Marc's orders!

Dinah swore fluently, summing up her reaction, so that she had Thalia grinning. 'You owe me,' said Dinah. 'All I want to do is go quietly. Where's the helicopter's next stop?'

The helicopter pad had a coating of muddy earth, but landing and take-off had been effected without mishap, and any time now the pilot was returning to Crete to collect supplies.

'If that's what you want,' said Thalia. She produced a lightweight bag, and Dinah packed in feverish haste. Once off Styros she could go to earth for a few days in Crete. She had hardly spent any money since she arrived here, and no one was expecting to see her back for at least another two weeks. However, if she could get a flight home sooner she might prefer to get into a working routine again. Any holiday mood had been well and truly dissipated, and the last thing she wanted was time to sit and think.

Thalia sat on the bed as Dinah dashed round the room. 'I'll change out of your dress,' said Dinah.

'Keep it,' said Thalia. 'Give it to Oxfam if you can't bear to wear it. I'm sorry I've been such a bitch.'

Dinah's smile slanted. 'You've a talent for it.'

'You, too. You don't get put down easily. If things had been different, we might have been friends.'

After a little thought, Dinah conceded, 'We might, at that.'

'Maybe, some time——' Thalia began.

'No,' interrupted Dinah firmly.

'Pity. But we'll look out for your photographs, and I hope you'll be lucky in everything.'

'If you mean men,' said Dinah, 'I've decided they're more trouble than they're worth.' She patted her camera case. 'I'm never alone with this.' And she scooped up the contents of the last drawer and crammed them into the bag, too.

Looking down from the helicopter, she could see the erratic path of the whirlwind, and she wondered where Marcus was. She could imagine him, shirtless, slogging down there, and she realised that she had packed his shirt with her luggage. If she had known where he was, and if they had passed overhead, she would have dropped it out and let it float down. Another souvenir of Styros she could do without. From now on she was set on forgetting them all. She was going home, and there at least she could control her own life.

She arrived in Heathrow that night, and phoned Barbara from an airport hotel. Thalia had given the helicopter pilot instructions that meant Dinah got VIP treatment all the way. A first-class seat was found for her on a plane leaving Heraklion, charged presumably to a Christophi account, and she saw no reason why not; it was their fault she was not using her own tourist return.

She booked into the first hotel that could take her, and rang Barbara. The tornado had made the end of the news, and Barbara had been anxious, although no loss of life had been reported and, as whirlwinds went, the Styros tornado was small-time. 'Bad, was it?' Barbara asked worriedly.

'Bad enough.'

'You are all right?'

'Never better.' Although it might have been nearer the truth if she had said that she'd never felt worse, because suddenly she was deeply depressed, as if running away had not been a good idea after all.

Next day she finished her journey home by train and taxi, drawing up more or less outside the studio in mid-afternoon. Barbara was out of the shop as Dinah picked up her case from the pavement, asking, 'Where's the Mini?' Presumably she hadn't had Dinah's letter yet.

'Lord knows,' said Dinah. 'I did for that on my way to Luton. I should have taken it as an omen, and stopped right there. I'm glad to see this place still standing. My luck's been hellish lately.'

Barbara followed her into the empty shop and through the door that led into the ground-floor bedsitter that had been Dinah's home since her father died. 'What's *happened*?' she was asking, and Dinah dumped Thalia's expensive-looking bag on the bed.

'It was a beautiful place, but the weather was weird, very, very heavy, building up to the tornado, I suppose, and Nic's family hardly welcomed me with open arms. Another heavy scene that got too much.'

Her smile was bright, she was almost laughing, but Barbara still looked concerned. 'I did take some photographs that might be earners, and I suppose I'd better be phoning about my car,' said Dinah.

'Start there,' said Barbara. 'Let's hear what happened to your car.'

Dinah told her, and Barbara made coffee and announced, 'You're coming to us for a meal tonight, and don't start arguing. Shall I help you unpack?'

'I'll do it,' Dinah said hastily. Anyone unpacking that bag would realise that she had left in a state of panic which she could not start explaining.

So she drank her coffee, and waited until Barbara had gone back into the shop before she unzipped and upended it, and began sorting the contents. She dragged out Marcus's shirt from the pile, and threw it across the room, where it landed draped over a chair. She got the rest into some order, with a bundle for the launderette, and then went into the shop to phone the garage where she had left her car.

It was about to be transferred to the wreckers' yard, they said, having been certified irreparable. So then she rang her insurance broker who was dealing with everything, alerted and encouraged by somebody in the Christophi legal department. 'Not Jack Cameron, by any chance?' said Dinah. No, the name was Prue Miller. Of course, Jack was the boy for the big deals, international hush-hush wheeler-dealer scene.

'Thank you,' Dinah said, putting down the phone.

'Well?' asked Barbara.

'It's all going through, the insurance and that. I told them about it when I got there and—er—Nic said they'd get on to it.'

She could not say Marc. Her lips would not frame his name, and she got through the long evening without mentioning him once, although she talked about Styros.

Barbara, flanked by her bank manager husband and art student son, dished up a casserole and said, 'Now we want to hear all about it.'

Dinah started with Lola and the magical potions and the bruises that weren't, and that had them smiling.

She described the villa and the lake and the fresco in the caves, the heaviness in the air and how the tornado came. She spoke of everyone but Marc. She even said, 'When things got sticky, it was Nic and Thalia, and that's when I realised I was the odd one out, so I hitched a lift off the island while the men were away from the villa.'

'I'm sorry,' said Barbara.

'You can't win them all,' said Dinah gaily. 'Those two were made for each other.' This time, Barbara relaxed, reassured that Dinah's heart was not breaking for Nic.

Barbara's husband gave Dinah a lift home, and she expected to sleep, but found herself, after midnight, standing in the middle of her bedroom, very wide awake. She was too restless to read, so she went into her darkroom and began developing the films from Styros.

She usually enjoyed this stage. Her pictures were rarely below standard, and these were no exception. The negatives were sharp and clear, and she clipped them and left them in the drying cabinet, clearing up and feeling she could sleep now after a job well done.

She lay in her divan bed against the wall, and thought how odd it was that moonlight should fall full on the chair over which that wretched shirt was draped, as if there was always something around to remind her of Marcus. She was not getting out of bed to remove it now but, 'In the morning,' she told it, 'I shall turn you into a floorcloth.'

In the morning, Dinah was up and dressed, drinking coffee in her kitchenette section and vaguely planning her day, when Barbara brought in the mail, collected from behind the shop door as she'd arrived for work. She put down a personal letter for Dinah, and an envelope that looked like a bank statement, then said 'I got a letter from you at home this morning.'

'Did you? Not from Styros?'

'From England. But you'd written it on Styros.'

Someone from the organisation must have been flying to England that day, and Dinah said tartly, 'Aren't they the efficient set-up? I wonder it wasn't hand-delivered. I bet it was censored. Had it been opened and resealed?'

'What?' gasped Barbara.

'Oh, but it could have been. Nic was on his way to get me a ring that morning. Big brother wasn't sure I wouldn't take it, but I can't see him passing up a chance to find out. Nobody knew then that the whirlwind was going to change Nic's ideas.'

'Would you?' asked Barbara.

Dinah replied without hesitation. 'No, I liked Nic. At times, I was sorry for him, and that's pretty stupid when you think about it. But I never really wanted to marry him.'

'Then what's bugging you?' asked Barbara. 'And who's big brother?'

'Thalia's brother. Nic's other cousin. I told you about him.'

'Before you went, yes. Not since you came back.'

'I'd rather talk about the weather,' said Dinah. 'Although that man and a tornado have something in common. It's safer out of their way.' She opened her bank statement and pulled a face. 'When I get the prints done, I'll know what I've salvaged from my holiday.'

Barbara was not going to follow her into the darkroom asking questions, and when Dinah called her to view the finished products her approval was warm and unstinted. 'You've got some beautiful shots here. I'm sure Phoebe will want them.' She stared at the men and the helicopter. 'Who are these?'

'The big one's Thalia's brother, he's Jack Cameron, a lawyer, and I don't know who the others are. They came to discuss a deal. They look important, don't they?'

Barbara grinned. 'They look like a gun-runner and a Mafia boss. What was the deal?'

'Nobody told me. It was top-secret. I was just snapping out of habit. I wasn't supposed to be there.'

'And that's big brother. Well, I think we should drop this and the negative to the bottom of a deep drawer and forget it.' Barbara was not sure herself whether she was joking, and neither was Dinah. 'That's Marcus again?' she said.

She was looking at the pictures of the little square, with the students, the cats sleeping in the sun, and Marcus at the table under the pepper tree. 'Isn't he something?' said Barbara, a loyal and loving wife, but appreciating male charisma when she saw it.

'Something else,' said Dinah in a very different tone.

She busied herself all day. Closing the shop and the studio at six o'clock, she went back to the photographs, selecting those for Phoebe and putting them in a folder. In her own room, she sat cross-legged on the floor, taking the personal photographs slowly.

She had developed another set of the Cornish shots, including the one of Nic in his studio. She might send that to Thalia some day. He looked handsome, with the wistful charm that was part of his appeal. Lola's face had strength and humour. Thalia was graceful as a relaxing dancer on the rock-ledge over the lake, and Dinah looked at them all for a long time.

She left the café shots till last. They all showed Marcus. Sometimes off-centre, sometimes turning away, but she had included him in the frame of every picture. And once full-face, his eyes watching under lazy lids.

When they had first met, she had thought he would be a difficult subject, that it would need more than her skill to strip his soul bare or show anything about him that was not general knowledge.

She held the picture at eye-level, searching for something, and, oh, how well she remembered how it was. The heat of the sun, the sounds around, her hand on his arm and his fingers covering hers as she'd told him, 'I'm enjoying myself so much.'

'I can't remember a better day,' he had said, and for her it had been a day like no other, because she had never fallen in love before.

Her hands were shaking. She put down the photograph, but she couldn't take her eyes off it. She leaned forwards, her hair tumbling over her face. 'Marcus,' she said softly, and again, 'Marc.'

She liked saying his name. It was the name of all names she liked best, just as from the beginning he had been the man who blotted out the rest. All her fury and frustration had been because he was against her when she desperately wanted him to stay her friend and ally. And lover. The only man she wanted to love her more than she wanted to go on living.

She gave herself up to the luxury of dreaming, recalling every tiny detail so that she was back in that square on that day, telling him again about adding up the good times to make one year of happiness. 'If I was doing that, I'd count all of today.'

'So would I,' he said, and his hand covered hers and his eyes were dark and steady. When he kissed her, she felt the warmth rippling through her from the sensuous pressure of his mouth.

She kissed him back, lightly because the square was crowded, and she said, 'I don't want to marry Nic.'

Marc said, 'I want you, I love you.'

'Yes,' she murmured joyfully.

Twice the phone rang in the shop, and she let it ring on until the callers gave up. She had never done much daydreaming before, but now she was into a fantasy world more erotic and exciting than anywhere between here and Styros.

Make-believe and memories. Remembering what had happened between herself and Marcus, taking the settings—under the moon in the mountains, the caves, the night of the rains, only no Thalia, just the two of them—and letting her imagination drift into how it would have been if they had been lovers.

The images in her mind had her gasping for breath, so that if he *had* taken her she might have gone up like tinder; but she wished it had happened. She was going to remember him for ever, and she wished she had left some room, some place, haunted for him. If they had made love, caring and passionate, he would not have found it so easy to forget her. He was a powerfully attractive man, and of course there were women in his life, but she did not believe he was promiscuous. He would have remembered her then.

But they had not, and the regret was probably all on her side. She could have been seduced, and that showed he was not a casual womaniser. It also proved he was not lusting after her, much less falling in love with her, and she looked at the photograph again and thought, I've as much chance as somebody mooning over a pop star. Except that I *do* have an address and an excuse to get in touch. I can send these photographs, for a start.

The phone rang again, and this time she went out to answer it. A girl she had gone to school with, who had just heard she was home, said, 'Karen here. You're back soon, aren't you?'

Dinah said the weather hadn't helped. Tornadoes rather put you off a villa up in the mountains. And no, the affair hadn't gone too well either, which was the next question Karen asked.

'Come to Cheltenham with me tomorrow for the day?' Dinah said all right, because there was no work waiting, and Karen usually chattered, so she wouldn't have to do much talking herself.

If she hung around here tomorrow, Barbara was sharp enough to spot something different in her. She needed a day at least to get used to the idea that she was in love for the very first time. And the last. That was the frightening part—that Marcus Christophi was the one she had been waiting for, but she knew he had not been waiting for her. And if she put on a cheerful face and smiled too much, or if she sighed, Barbara would want to know why.

Barbara had always been like a youngish aunt, and Dinah looked at herself in a long, oval mirror on the wall of her bedsitter, examining her reflection for how Barbara might see her. She looked calm enough. But then she thought of Marc—she didn't even say his name, she just thought of him—and her cheeks pinked and her eyes shone, and she knew that Barbara would not need a truth mirror to get at the truth.

She remembered Lola's mirror, and Thalia standing behind her, asking, 'Do you love Nic more than you could love any other man?' That had touched a raw nerve because, if Dinah had answered honestly, the answer would have been,

'Marcus is the man who could keep me faithful for ever.'

She said it now, and it was no comfort. It could mean that she would grow old unloved, or settle for second best somewhere along the way. Both seemed too awful to contemplate. She shivered and picked up the shirt, clutching it to her, and the feel of it brought back that first night, when she had wept over her smashed case, and he had put his arms around her and strength had flowed into her.

She needed strength now. She should never have run away, she should have stayed on Styros, and when she saw him again she should have said, 'I'm glad for Nic and Thalia.' She could have made friends with Thalia and been close to Marc. Of all the stupid, impetuous moves she had ever made, getting into that helicopter had been the craziest.

She should have realised sooner that she was mad about him, not waited until she was all alone back home, with nothing but his shirt and his photograph and his voice on a tiny tape. But on Styros she had been mixed up. Perhaps she had needed to get away to think clearly, and it was no use wishing herself on Styros again.

She could dream, but in real life she was here, and from here she had to come up with some way of getting herself back into Marcus Christophi's life.

She took the shirt to bed with her, stroking it on the pillow beside her. If she dreamt, she couldn't remember, but she woke hugging it and missing him. She had wondered if she might feel different in the morning, but her first thoughts were of Marcus. This had never happened to her before with any other man, this longing that suffused her so that she didn't know whether to laugh or cry.

In the end, she did neither. She sat up, sniffed, put the shirt aside and threw back the sheets. She had never shared that single divan with anyone, but she could almost believe that she had shared it with him last night.

She was waiting for Barbara to arrive, dressed for the weather, which promised another fine day. She had dealt with the mail, so there was nothing to keep her, and she greeted Barbara with 'It's all right if I take the day off and go shopping, isn't it? I'll get down to work tomorrow.'

'Take two or three days,' said Barbara affably. 'You're still supposed to be on holiday.' The phone rang then, and she said, 'I'll get it.'

'Expect me when you see me,' called Dinah, and walked off briskly towards Karen's home, a bungalow on the outskirts of town, where she lived with her parents.

Karen was a temping secretary, between jobs, a blonde, bubbly girl who rarely stopped talking. She had just brought her car out of the garage, parking it in front of the house, and when she saw Dinah she got out of the driving seat, her lips moving before Dinah could hear the words.

'Sorry about your Mini,' she was saying. Dinah had told her about the accident on the phone last night, and Karen started recounting something similar that had happened to her once, although Dinah had heard the tale many times before.

As they drove away, Karen asked, 'What happened with the gorgeous man?'

'We both had second thoughts,' said Dinah. 'How is it with you?'

Karen liked hearing the gossip, but she was happiest talking about herself, and today Dinah did not mind at all. Karen was easier to be with right now than Barbara would have been.

They wandered through the shops in the Regency Arcade, looking, discussing, occasionally buying. And although Dinah knew her own style, what suited her and what she wanted, for the first time she was shopping with a man in mind. When she tried on a flame-coloured

dress that looked stunning, she thought, he's got to see
me in this. With Karen twittering on, she wrote out a
cheque for more than she could afford.

She rarely stopped thinking about him that day.
Midday, they stood among the shoppers who gathered
under the fantasy clock, a fairy-tale whimsy high above.
As the hours struck, the goose laid the golden egg, and
a brief pantomime continued. A tune tinkled, 'I'm for
ever blowing bubbles,' and, from the mouth of a brightly
painted fish, rainbow bubbles floated down. A child in
his father's arms reached for one, and it vanished at a
touch. The child shrieked, and the father said, 'That's
life, son.' Dinah thought, sometimes, surely, a dream
comes true?

Late afternoon, they sat at the table outside a restaurant, and a man who towered over the rest walked
by; Dinah watched him. It was another way in which
Marc had changed her ideas. A tall, broad-shouldered
man could make her smile now, just because he reminded her of Marc. 'Hey,' said Karen, observant for
once, 'do you fancy him?'

Dinah shook her head, still smiling. Not any of them,
she could have said.

It had been a pleasant day, and it lasted longer than
they had planned, when a young couple, going into the
delicatessen at the back of the café, hailed them at their
table.

They all knew each other. The shopping was for a
buffet party tonight in the couple's flat, to which Dinah
and Karen were promptly invited.

The party went on into the small hours. Karen got
merry on home-made wine, and was persuaded to stay
overnight. That was fine by Dinah, who had no one
waiting for her.

Nights had never been lonely for Dinah. They had been for sleeping, but now it could be different. In the dark hours she might have to face the possibility that she was never going to see Marc again or, even if she did, he would always be beyond her reach. From now on, nights could be unbearably lonely.

She accepted a sleeping-bag gratefully, and curled up on a settee. And next morning, she helped with the clearing up while Karen drank black coffee before driving home, pale and silent for once, around lunch time.

Dinah, carrying her parcels, let herself into the shop, and Barbara came bustling up, gasping, 'Am I glad to see you! They're after you.'

'Who?' Dinah quipped gaily. 'The law? Vatman?'

'I hope it's funny,' said Barbara. 'The Christophis.'

Dinah's heart started racing, and her throat was suddenly dry as dust. 'What for?'

'A business talk.' Barbara made that sound very sinister.

'What sort of business? Who was it? What did they say?'

Barbara turned the 'Open' sign hanging behind the glass panel of the door to 'Closed', and slipped on the latch. Then she headed for the studio, explaining as she went, 'There was a phone call for you yesterday. I said you weren't here, and wouldn't be for the rest of the day at least, and could I take a message.' Inside the studio, she shut that door too, and turned to Dinah. 'They want you at Cheslyn Grange this evening, any time after six o'clock, for a business talk.'

'*Who* does?'

'Marcus Christophi.' Dinah felt as if she had stepped into a liftshaft when the lift wasn't there. Barbara had the helicopter picture on the table. 'You don't think it's got anything to do with this?' She was whispering, as if the walls had ears. 'This top-secret deal when you weren't supposed to be taking photographs? You didn't hear anything, or find out anything?'

Dinah tried to laugh. 'You've been watching too many thrillers.' But she had heard snatches of phone calls, she *had* been around while something was going on. Marcus had spotted her taking this picture, and then suggested she handed over the film. And given orders she was not to leave the villa.

'And look at this,' said Barbara. Also on the table was the business section from a newspaper. 'Every other story seems to be about corporate take-overs and insider dealings. I don't understand any of it, but there *is* this photograph and you *are* a free-lance with press connections. Can you think of any other business they'd be wanting to discuss in a hurry?'

She looked hard at Marc's picture, declaring, 'He could be Mr Big, behind—well—anything.'

He certainly looked the part, and Dinah tried to laugh again and introduce a lighter note. 'Nic wanted to give me a gold bracelet and an engagement ring. It wasn't an engagement ring by then, but his conscience was bothering him. Thalia might have gift-wrapped them and sent them over. I told her she owed me, and we were getting quite matey when we said goodbye.'

She was babbling like Karen and Barbara asked flatly, 'Would he be bringing them?'

Of course not. Dinah said, 'He was pleased Nic came to his senses, that took a weight off his shoulders, but he wouldn't be bringing me goodies.'

Barbara drew in a sharp breath, but after a few moments she said, 'Well, there should be plenty of people around. You should be safe enough.'

'I should hope so.'

'You *are* going?'

'Of course I'm going.' Dinah picked up the photograph and wondered again who they were; she was quite glad she didn't know. 'If they want this, they can have it, and if they think I know anything they can rely on my discretion, because I've no idea what it is.'

Barbara was hoping all this was far-fetched, that it was simply her imagination running wild. She made a little joke. 'He could make you an offer you can't refuse.' Over Dinah's shoulder, she took another look at Marcus Christophi, and added quite seriously, 'But if it was me, I'd just hand it over. I shouldn't want to make an enemy of him.'

It seemed long ago since Dinah had thought of Marc as her enemy. Just seeing his photograph now turned her bones to water. When she went to meet him tonight, he could be flanked by others. Or her appointment could be with someone else. Maybe Jack Cameron had summoned her yesterday, in Marc's name, on Marc's orders.

But between now and then she would pamper herself into the best she had ever looked, hoping that when she walked into the foyer of Cheslyn Grange, at six o'clock sharp, Marc would be waiting for her, and alone.

She booked a taxi. She did not want Barbara driving her there, she did not want anyone with her when she arrived.

Cheslyn Grange had once been a rambling, early-Victorian house. Now it was a super-smart country club. This evening the car park was filling, the tennis courts had a full quota of players, and through wide windows the swimming pool looked almost as popular.

This was where it had all started. That night she had been so sure of herself. Confident and content. Meeting Nicholas had been fun. Her feelings for him had been warm and happy and tender, but they had not prepared her for this.

Nothing in her whole life had prepared her for the hunger that possessed her now, so fiercely that she could have fainted. She sat on a stone seat and looked down at her clenched hands.

Marc could be waiting for her, and that scared her. Or he might not be there, and that would be a bitter blow. She had to go in, find out and take it from there. Sitting here was doing no good, and she almost walked off, leaving her bag behind. She turned back and slung the strap over her shoulder, then strode into the reception area, chin up.

The fashion show had been held here on opening night, the models coming down the wide staircase from the upper gallery. Tonight it was less crowded, but there were plenty of folk around and movement everywhere.

He got up from an armchair in a lounge leading off the hall. The door was open, so he had been watching for her, and she saw him at once, as though all the rest were shadows. No one came with him, he was alone, and she had to remind herself to walk slowly and smile nicely. Don't rush at him, or he'll think you've gone off your head.

He looked, as always, the most impressive man in the place. His dark grey suit was superbly cut. But it was not the clothes. He would cause as much stir dressed like a tramp, and she desperately wanted to touch him. 'Hello,' she said with a bright smile.

'Thank you for coming.' When they parted, she had been shouting, and he had told her not to be childish, so he couldn't have known she would smile when she saw him. He took her hand and she pulled away, because if she hadn't she never would have done.

She said gaily, 'Barbara didn't seem to think I had much choice. She said it sounded urgent. What she actually said was, ''The Christophis are after you.''' He laughed at that, and she asked, 'What is it all about?'

'Shall we discuss it in private?'

He led her towards a lift, ornate as a golden birdcage. They had an apartment in this place. Nic had slept here, but the décor and the furnishings had been unfinished when the club opened. Dinah had eaten in the restaurant, but she had never been up here before. Another couple in the lift went on with their conversation, but the woman's eyes were on Marc.

On the top floor, he opened a door and said, 'I'd rather this wasn't overheard.'

'Our business talk?'

'Exactly.'

So, Barbara could have been right, it could have something to do with secrets and the photographs she carried in her shoulder-bag.

'Nice place,' she said inanely.

Probably the best apartment there was, overlooking the gardens, with squashy leather furniture and the impression of being designer-created. 'Do sit down.'

She sat on a sofa, that being the nearest, and said, 'Thank you.' Marcus poured two glasses of white wine, and she accepted hers because, although she must keep a clear head, it was easier to act nonchalant if you had a wineglass to play with.

He took a chair. 'You left very suddenly,' he said.

Thalia might have told him how she had rammed everything into that bag and run, how nothing could have stopped her. 'It seemed a good idea,' Dinah said. She took a sip of wine. 'How were things?'

'A lot of damage. Repairs will take time. But nobody killed or seriously hurt, and that's the main thing.'

'How was the lake? The fresco?'

'The water was high, but so is that cave. I haven't been down again, but I feel that the wildcat is still there.'

She hoped so. She was almost sure herself. 'You should have let me photograph it,' she said.

'How did the photographs come out?' he asked.

'I thought you'd like to see them.' She picked up the bag. They were all in here, and the tapes. She handed him the photographs, with the helicopter shot at the bottom of the pile, and watched as he examined them.

'Yes, indeed,' he said. 'They're excellent.'

Not by a flicker did he show any more interest in the big-deal men than in the study of Lola or the café cats. Not that she had thought he would. She asked, 'What did you want to see me about?'

'I want you to do some promotional photography for me.' She would, of course, for it would be a real professional break, but she would have taken on anything that got her back into his orbit.

He could be offering her the commission as compensation for losing Nic. He could know she was good and hope she would do it well, although until now she doubted if he had seen much of her work.

Or it could be a way to keep her quiet about the things she had heard and seen. She said, 'I think I might know why.'

He was still holding the photograph, and he looked up at her with grim amusement. 'I thought you might.'

'It's something to do with what they came to discuss with you. The hush-hush deal or takeover, or whatever it is. And maybe you think I overheard something or got something on my tapes. They're in here, too.' She tipped them out of the bag, on to the sofa. 'You don't want that picture getting any publicity, do you?'

'This one?' He put it down on a low table beside him. 'Not very good of Jack, and I never was photogenic, but speaking for the others I should say you could paste it on bill-boards for all they'd care. Who do you think they are?'

She shook her head. 'Two members of my board,' he said. 'Old colleagues and old friends.'

She babbled, 'Not a gun-runner and a Mafia boss?' She had made an idiot of herself again and he was laughing at her.

'Sorry. No.' She jumped up, and he said 'Sit down.'

Dinah felt so ridiculous that she snapped, 'Don't little-woman me!'

'Then don't big-man me.' He was not laughing. He sounded as though somebody should be shaking her. 'And for God's sake stop being so suspicious. Whoever he was who underpaid your father for his property, that was years ago. If he'd had a moustache, would you have distrusted men with moustaches for the rest of your life?' He stood up, towering over her, pushing her down on to the settee. She went back against the soft leather cushions and stayed there, staring up, and he sat down again in the chair and said harshly, 'I don't know what I'm going to do with you if you won't let me touch you.'

'Do you want to touch me?'

He leaned forwards, speaking slowly and distinctly as if what he was saying was obvious but they did not speak the same language. 'Your work is good. These photographs are good. But the world's full of good photographers, and the only reason I'm trying to recruit you is because I want you where I can see you and touch you and make love to you.'

She heard herself say 'What?' although she knew what she had heard.

'You didn't realise that? Or at least have some idea?' He sounded surprised.

She shook her head. She had been aware from the beginning what he was doing to her, but not how she might be affecting him.

'Does the prospect appal you?' He was controlled, eyes and voice steady, and she could hardly say, I'm burning up for you, I'm on fire, when he was so cool.

She merely said, 'No.'

'That's a start. Why did you leave Styros?'

'I told you, it seemed a good idea.'

'Nic wouldn't have been right for you.'

'Because of Thalia?'

'I think they'll do well together, but that wasn't why I couldn't let him marry you.'

She wanted his arms around her and his mouth on hers, but she wanted to hear this, too. She didn't move a muscle. She was hardly breathing, drinking in the words as he told her, 'At first, I thought if you came to Styros you'd find out if it was just infatuation. Get to know each other, for better or worse. The message came that you were on your way, and I let Nic go because I wanted to see you for myself again. Make another assessment, without prejudice.'

His smile was wry and self-mocking. 'Only, of course, it was nothing to do with Nic. I wanted to see you alone. And I knew as soon as I saw you again that you were for me.'

Yes, she thought, yes...

'The day we went to meet the *Condor*, you were all I needed,' he said. 'When you said you were happy, I wanted to be the one to make you happy.' She looked into eyes that were desperate and pleading. 'I can do that,' he said. 'Believe me, I can.'

She leaned across to touch his arm, and again she felt the strength of his fingers closing over hers. That day, she had known where she belonged, known the man she wanted to be with. She said, 'I never said I'd marry Nic. I hadn't given him an answer, only he couldn't remember that, either.'

Marc waited. Now it was his turn to hold his breath. When she said, 'It would have been no,' he smiled slowly, a smile that started in his eyes and softened the harsh lines of his face as he asked her,

'Why, in heaven's name, didn't you say so?'

She smiled, too. 'Because you riled me, and I thought he needed protecting against you.' That made her laugh, but then she was serious. 'If it had been the real thing, I would have stayed at that hospital, I would have seen him.'

If Marc was hurt or ill, nobody would be able to keep her from him, and he said, 'Yes,' and she knew that he would be there whenever she needed him.

That was a miracle, and she said huskily, 'If I had told you, I might not have been invited to Styros.'

He was sitting beside her, holding her gently. 'You wouldn't have got away. I've been waiting for you for a long time.'

He kissed her, gently at first, and then as she had never been kissed before. Her heart was hammering and the heat of desire was firing the whole surface of her body, reaching deep and molten within as the urge to possess him possessed her.

At first she couldn't hear what he said above the roaring in her ears. But he wasn't kissing her now. Holding her, yes, but without the savage passion that had nearly had her tearing clothes to reach the ultimate closeness.

'Would you like the wildcat in gold or white gold?' he said.

'Would I what?' She must stop saying 'what?' when she had heard what was said.

'The wildcat,' he repeated. 'I'm having a brooch made for you.'

'Thank you.' That came out jerkily, because a pulse in her throat was fluttering fit to choke her. Her face was flaming and so, probably, was every inch of her body. It seemed he could just switch off, but she had been turned on as never before, and she needed time to adjust. She pressed her hands to her hot cheeks and tried deep breathing.

Marc got up, crossed the room, picking up a memo pad and coming back with it to sit in the chair, not the sofa. 'That's it, isn't it?' he said.

The sketch was the cat, and a brooch would be nice, but surely this discussion could have waited? She said, 'It's an exact copy. Did you draw it?'

'You and I are the only ones who've seen it. I only found it a few weeks ago. Nobody else knows about it.'

He had shown it to her and no one else. That had been a marvellous secret to share! She said, 'Lord, I hope the floods didn't wash it away.'

'I'll feel guilty if they did. It's an archaeological find. It should have been reported.'

Suddenly, she was sure it was safe, as safe as she would be from this day on. He was telling her, 'The caves have always been a secret world for me. I found the way in when I was a boy. Archaeologists came afterwards, but that was over twenty years ago. In recent years, I've mostly gone down alone.' He was sitting well back in his chair, smiling at her, and she loved him so. 'You're the one I want to share them with. I want to share everything with you.'

She wanted that, so why were they talking when she was aching for him? Her dress had slipped from one shoulder and she sat up, lifting her hair from her glowing face, her breasts rising and falling because she was still breathing deeply, although it was not making her calmer, only breathless.

'Would you mind not doing that?' he said.

'What?' There she went again. 'Doing what?'

'Looking like that.' His voice was deep and slow, as always, but with a rough edge to it. 'I'm trying to behave in a civilised fashion. If you have no idea how I feel about you, you may need time to get used to it. But when you look like that I find it almost impossible to keep my hands off you.' His strong, brown hands were clasped, and his knuckles showed white. 'And the way I'm feeling just now, a touch could well be the point of no return.'

She let out all her breath in one gasp, gulped in air again and almost shrieked, 'Who's asking you to act civilised?'

There was a moment of silence, then she looked into his eyes and stood up as he stood; as she closed her eyes she felt his arms around her, his lips on the smooth skin of her shoulder. 'One other thing——' he said.

'Oh, *no!*'

'I want you to marry me.' Her eyes flew open at that, not in surprise, but to see his face. 'And don't say that's the first you've heard of that, because I told you before.'

So he had, and on a deep level of her subconscious she had never stopped thinking of how it would be.

He said, 'I'm not a possessive man. Other men can look at you, they always will. But I want my ring on your finger.'

'Do other men look at me? Coming up in the lift just now, that woman couldn't take her eyes off you.'

'I wasn't aware of that. But I did see the man looking at you. And it wasn't the red dress—it always happens.'

She laughed a little at the thought of him jealous for her, and because they were so right for each other. She said, 'Barbara said you might make me an offer I couldn't refuse. She was thinking of the photograph. She didn't mean the offer I'm getting!'

'About the offer...' he said. He gathered her up in his arms, and she laced her fingers behind his head, then he carried her into another room, where the bed was cool and wide, and there was tonight and a lifetime ahead for them to discover all the best and beautiful reasons why she could never say no.

Harlequin Temptation dares to be different!

Once in a while, we Temptation editors spot a romance that's truly innovative. To make sure *you* don't miss any one of these outstanding selections, we'll mark them for you.

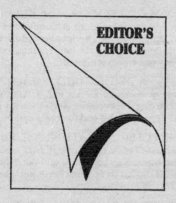

EDITOR'S
CHOICE

When the "Editors' Choice" fold-back appears on a Temptation cover, you'll know we've found that extra-special page-turner!

THE

Temptation

EDITORS

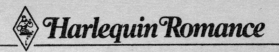
Harlequin Romance

Coming Next Month

2959 PAINTED LADY Diana Hamilton
Ziggy, reunited with her grandfather in England, revises her opinion of him and the family feud that separated them. But she won't change her opinion of Rafe d'Anjou. She's sure his interest in bringing her and her grandfather together, and in herself, is entirely selfish.

2960 ONLY MY DREAMS Rowan Kirby
A true romantic and dreamer, Erinna is furious when her staid Midlands tutor, Dr. John Bryce, cautions her against taking life at face value. What does he know, she fumes, a man seemingly impervious to any real emotion himself!

2961 ALWAYS A BRIDESMAID Patricia Knoll
Shelby Featherstone wants store space in A. J. Court's exclusive San Diego mall—not a ring on her finger. And especially not the heartache of having to plan his real fiancée's wedding!

2962 STORM CLOUDS GATHERING Edwina Shore
Everyone is keen to tell Jenna that Drew Merrick is back on the Australian island where they both grew up—but nobody can tell her why. Certainly it's the last thing Jenna needs just when she's made up her mind to marry Adam.

2963 YESTERDAY'S ENEMY Lee Stafford
Ten years ago Steve Rodriguez had deprived Nicole's stepfather of his livelihood, so it's ironic when her job lands her back at the scene of the crime. Will Steve recognize her as "young Nicky"? And if he does, how should she react?

2964 WITHOUT LOVE Jessica Steele
Kassia lost her job because of Lyon Mulholland, who even blocked her subsequent efforts to get another one. So her feelings for him bordered on hatred. Yet when he makes handsome amends, she finds her troubles are only just starting....

Available in February wherever paperback books are sold, or through Harlequin Reader Service:

In the U.S.
901 Fuhrmann Blvd.
P.O. Box 1397
Buffalo, N.Y. 14240-1397

In Canada
P.O. Box 603
Fort Erie, Ontario
L2A 5X3

ATTRACTIVE, SPACE SAVING BOOK RACK

Display your most prized novels on this handsome and sturdy book rack. The hand-rubbed walnut finish will blend into your library decor with quiet elegance, providing a practical organizer for your favorite hard-or soft-covered books.

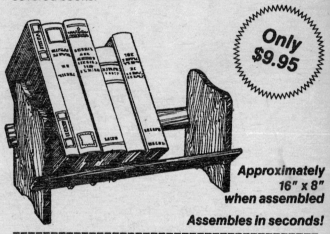

Only $9.95

Approximately 16" x 8" when assembled

Assembles in seconds!

To order, rush your name, address and zip code, along with a check or money order for $10.70* ($9.95 plus 75¢ postage and handling) payable to *Harlequin Reader Service*:

Harlequin Reader Service
Book Rack Offer
901 Fuhrmann Blvd.
P.O. Box 1396
Buffalo, NY 14269-1396

Offer not available in Canada.

BKR-1A

*New York and Iowa residents add appropriate sales tax.